CAIN

AND THE

MOUNTAIN

Alan McClure

Callum and the Mountain

First published 2019 by Beaten Track Publishing

Paperback ISBN: 978 1 78645 326 6
eBook ISBN: 978 1 78645 327 3

Cover design by Roe Horvat

Beaten Track Publishing,
Burscough, Lancashire.
www.beatentrackpublishing.com

For Fergus and Robin

Contents

CALLUM
AND THE
MOUNTAIN

Part 1

School

Here's a scene, look: twelve-year-old Callum Maxwell, bored and distracted, gazing from his treehouse at the wee town below. A light breeze is making the leaves rustle round him, and now and again the peely-wally sunlight breaks through the clouds. It almost makes the town look pretty, but our Callum, he's in no mood to notice. Every detail makes him cross.

An old car puttering up Main Street from the harbour? *Ach!*

The dog barking in Mr. McKendrick's garden? *Yawn!* Not even funny when Mr. McKendrick yells, "SHUT IT, you!" and the dog barks all the more frantically. (Well, maybe a *wee* bit funny.)

Three sparrows fighting in the leaves below him, a furious flurry of brown feathers and attitude? "Oh, gie's peace!" mutters Callum, a phrase he's learned from Papa and likes to air from time to time.

No, there's no inspiration in this scene, nothing to light a fire in the mind of a young genius like our hero. The town, he decides, is a painful disappointment and everyone in it bears the blame—don't they know they have a super-brain in their midst? Can't they make some *effort* to be interesting? *How,* reflects Callum bitterly, *am I supposed to be brilliant in a place like this?*

There's nothing for it: they need taught a lesson.

Motivated for the first time this morning, Callum snaps a long, green twig from the branch above him and carefully pinches off the leaves. "I'm sorry it's come to this," he mutters, "but you've only yourselves to blame." In Callum's clever fingers, the twig becomes a terrifying weapon—a gun of awesome power, fuelled only by the frazzling channels of energy which Callum imagines buzzing through his immense brain. *All I need to do is point, aim and fire. THEN you'll all be sorry!*

By this point, you'll have decided that Callum is a boy with a fertile imagination—perhaps, to be polite, just a touch on the glaikit side—and to be fair, Callum would be the first to admit this. If caught in an act of silly make-believe, he is quick to laugh at himself, or if the audience is right (if it's Craig or Vicky or Steven, for example) quick to include you in the fun. He's a good lad. And he knows, of course, that he's not *really* a genius, not *really* possessed of incredible powers.

So you can imagine his surprise when, on aiming the gun at the empty school, narrowing his eyes, purposefully pushing his ginger fringe back from his face and pulling his imaginary trigger, he is immediately walloped backwards by the force of an immense explosion. He batters into the back wall of the treehouse, knocking clean through it, and crashes through the branches to the grass below. Constellations of stars dance and fizz in his eyes, and in his ears is a shrieking, ringing cacophony. Then rubble starts to fall—wee chunks at first, falling like spring rain, then great lumps of concrete and asphalt cannonballing down, and Callum has to scrabble to the tree trunk to avoid being brained.

Coughing and spluttering in the gathering dust cloud, Callum's back to his senses enough to hear car alarms howling and voices raised in fury and surprise. There's already the banshee wail of fire engines—oh, and if Mr. McKendrick's dog was excited before it's pure *demented* now.

Well now, poor Callum's like jelly. He struggles to his feet. He can't quite keep up with what's just happened. Looking dumbly around at the wreckage, he notices that he's still clutching the green twig.

"Well," he says out loud. "*That* worked a lot better than I was expecting!" Then a great black cloud descends on his senses and he's tapselteerie face-first in the grass.

He passes out too quickly to notice that, up in the shaking branches of the hazel tree, a quick green figure is grinning down at him. It raises its arms, grasps a branch and swings itself up into nothingness, leaving only the certain fizz of mischief and the uncomfortable fact that mysterious things are afoot.

And whispering through the empty air, a breath a-hiss with glee—"*See you later, Callum Maxwell!*"— and a vanishing cackle from a time and place unknown, for now, to our hero.

Papa

Mystery Blast Rocks Town!

It's the only thing anyone can talk about for days, the mystery of the exploding school. The fact that it's exploded is strange enough, you might think, but as the investigations go on, the facts just keep getting weirder.

First off: although the whole school has absolutely definitely exploded, leaving a big hole where it once stood, none of the actual *pieces* of the school are damaged at all. Sure, they're scattered across a wide area, but every brick, every tile, even every *windowpane* managed to sail through the sky and land somewhere in the town without so much as a dent. When rebuilding begins, all they'll have to do is gather the stuff back up and put it together like a big jigsaw.

That, you may be sure, has folk scratching their heads.

Second up: although it was a Saturday and many people were out and about, nobody was even slightly hurt in the explosion. Dumfounert, certainly; flabbergasted, flummoxed and vexed. But even folk who were knocked off their feet—even *Callum,* who, as you'll remember, fell out of a tree—well, they all just got back up again without a scratch on them. Everybody's relieved about this, of course, but it just doesn't make sense.

Third—and you'd better brace yourself for this—on the morning after the explosion, Farmer McKenzie went up in his helicopter to take a photo in the morning light, and when he got home and printed it out, well, he nearly fainted. You see, the hole left where the school stood is almost perfectly round, and the debris scattered around the circle spells out a message. There's no doubt about it, it's writing—although at first no-one can understand it.

It says, *fàilte, coigreach!*

Gibberish, no?

No!

Now, not all of this information is made public because the people who make things public don't like the unexplained. For the time being, the blast is being blamed on a gas explosion, with Provost Kennedy making a public announcement in the town hall on Sunday afternoon.

"Here, how come there's no sign of fire damage?" asks Mrs. Watson from the paper shop.

The provost coughs, shuffles some papers and says, "Em, the gas must have burnt too fast to cause any charring, Mrs. Watson."

Folk aren't too convinced, especially when Dr. Harrison points out that the school wasn't even connected to the gas. All the power came from the turbine on the roof (which, by the way, landed undamaged in the play park making a great new roundabout for the kids to spin on).

"There *must* have been a connection *somewhere*," splutters the Provost, "otherwise there couldn't have been a gas explosion, could there?"

Well, if that's the kind of logic they're going to use, no-one wants to hear much more, so they all wander home to make up their own minds. But *you* know, of course, who blames himself for what happened. Poor Callum can't decide whether to go to the police and give himself up, tell his dad and risk a skelping, or confide in his pals, who will either think he's gone doolally or carry him shoulder high round the town for getting them all off school a week before the summer holidays were due to start.

So he does what he often does when he can't decide what to do. He goes to visit his Papa.

Papa doesn't keep as well as he used to. Up until a year or two ago, he would still go out walking on the mountain that holds Skerrils in its rocky lap, a landscape he knew better than anyone from his days as a ghillie on the estate. He's outlasted five estate owners and could show you every trout pool, every buzzard's nest, every heather-bound nook and cranny you could want to explore. Folk say Papa was never too hard on poachers, as long as they didn't take too much; if they did, they'd best watch out. But he's old now, and has trouble walking, so he sits by the window in a wee cottage at the bottom of the town, smoking a pipe and drinking strong tea.

"It's yourself, Callum," he says as his grandson enters the room. "Have some tea and sit yourself down. What's the good word?" This is Papa's way of asking for any news.

Callum pours himself a cup of tea from the pot on the stove, adds milk and three sugars, sits down and gets to the point.

"I blew up the school, Papa," he says.

Papa leans forward with a sparkle in his eyes. The light from the window is making his wispy hair look like a silvery halo round his chestnut-brown head, and he sooks appreciatively on his pipe with an air of great interest. "Tell me more, laddie," he says, wreaths of smoke curling up from his mouth, and Callum tells him everything.

When he's told the whole story, he says, "You'll probably say it's just a coincidence, but it honestly happened just the way I imagined. Well, apart from all the weird stuff about the writing and that."

Papa has listened intently, but at this, his ears prick up even further. "Writing, you say?"

"Aye, you must have heard? There was writing around the crater, Farmer McKenzie got it in his photo! Here. Look, his son Roy wrote it down for me!" Callum reaches into his pocket and pulls out a scrap of paper. Papa scans it. "Does it mean anything, Papa?"

Now, Callum's Papa is an old, old man, one of the last folk in the town to have lived there since the days when Gaelic was spoken. In some parts of Scotland, it's spoken yet, and there are places where the road signs are in Gaelic and they teach it in the school. But down here in Skerrils, no-one's really bothered and it's more or less disappeared.

But not quite.

"Aye, Callum, it means something," grins Papa. "It means it wasn't you who blew up the school. It means somebody's trying to get your attention, that's all."

Callum gasps. "Why, what does it say?" he whispers.

Papa leans back in his chair with a deeply satisfied sigh, the sigh of a man whose life has just gotten interesting again.

"It means 'Hello, stranger!'" he chuckles.

Normality

The strangest thing about strange things is how quickly they stop seeming strange. No doubt you imagine that after a few days of mystery, the good people of Skerrils will have risen in revolt, run the havering provost out of town and called in someone more sensible to figure it all out.

But in fact, the opposite is true. Fewer and fewer people seem bothered about what's happened. Builders have started gathering up the wreckage of the school in preparation for the rebuild, the gas-explosion theory has been more or less accepted, and the last few folk willing to make a fuss are taken about as seriously as those people who think aliens kidnap them to do experiments on their bottoms. Even Callum has his doubts now, strengthened by the reaction of his friends, which can be summed up in two words:

"Aye, *right.*"

Even if they had believed him, the *main* point of the school explosion is clearly not who did it, but the fact that they have an extra week of holiday and the sun is shining. So the three of them, Craig, Vicky and

Steven, are all cracking on with more important things. It doesn't stop Callum trying to persuade them, mind.

Here's Steven then, blonde and freckled, busy as always with his endless mission to build himself a boat. No-one quite remembers when Steven first had this idea, but over the years, it's become an obsession. Steven is determined to build a vessel that will carry him over the bay to MacArthur's Island.

"What about the writing? How do you explain that?" Callum asks from the rock he's sitting on. He's overlooking Steven's latest workshop—a wee pebbly beach scattered with driftwood and scraps of old rope. Steven is gazing thoughtfully at this flotsam and jetsam, imagining the swift, seaworthy vessel it will shortly become. He answers distractedly.

"Well, Max said he did that, didn't he?"

Callum snorts. "Max talks out his bum. Max says he invented the word 'skellington.'"

"Maybe he did." Steven's lack of interest rather stifles Callum's own, and in any case, the sea is sparkling like gold leaf and boat-building is more fun than puzzling over mysteries.

"What's the plan this time, then?" asks Callum, happy enough to think of something else for a bit.

"Catamaran," replies Steven solemnly.

It is the secretly held belief of all Steven's friends that if he sinks many more boats in his efforts to reach

MacArthur's Island, he'll be able just to walk across over the wreckage, but Callum doesn't say this. Instead, he asks, "How are you going to waterproof this one?"

Steven's eyes light up. "Follow me!" he says.

So Callum jumps onto the pebbles with a musical clatter, and they crunch around the coast for a bit, following the tideline.

Before long, Callum finds his senses arrested by an overwhelming smell. At first, he thinks it's just rotting seaweed, but as they continue, it gets stronger and stronger until Callum can hardly breathe without boaking.

"*Bleuch!*" he wheezes. "What the heck *is* that? It smells worse than the Trog's oxters!"

The Trog, if you're wondering, is a strange, wild man who is rumoured to stay in a cave around the coast from Skerrils, living off shellfish, performing strange rituals and probably not washing very thoroughly.

Steven, who has never really believed the stories of the Trog, answers rather abruptly. "*You* smell worse than the Trog's oxters. Now, come on—it's just a wee bit further!" And he marches forward as if there's nothing wrong.

At last, they arrive in a secluded inlet, and Callum's eyes are watering with the stink. He's also dismayed to hear a tremendous buzzing of flies. What is Steven doing?

"Look!" says Steven proudly, and he points at the shore. There, in a tangle of kelp and old fishing nets, is the bloated, foosty corpse of an unfortunate cow. Cattle do slip from the cliffs from time to time and get washed ashore—everyone knows this happens—but Steven would appear to be the first person to believe that the sad result is a tourist attraction.

Callum's insides are heaving. "What do you want *that* for?" he gasps.

Steven looks cross. "*Waterproofing,* of course!" His tone suggests that he thinks Callum an eejit for not figuring this out. "Leather, you see? That's what the old saints used to make their coracles. I just need to strip this and tan it and we'll be laughing!" Actually, Callum's laughing already.

"Jeez-oh," he gasps, "you'll die of the plague before you even start! That is pure, *pure* bogging, Steven!"

A short argument follows, Callum gently leading them away from the grisly scene to fresher pastures, and at last Steven is persuaded; cow corpses are not ideal boat-building materials. Callum bids him a cheery farewell, leaving him to think of another method of waterproofing.

It'll hopefully be better than his last attempt. About three months ago, he'd built a boat out of an old wooden packing crate and some fishing buoys and had found an old bucket of tar left over from some long-forgotten roadworks. He'd melted this over a bonfire and merrily painted his boat with a thick, sticky layer of it, inside and out. Convinced he was about to achieve his dream, he'd not had the patience to wait for the tar to dry, instead pushing boldly into the glittering sea with a homemade paddle and a look of determination on his face. After he'd paddled out about twenty metres (quite a good record, for him), the boat began to sink, as they always did. Steven, experienced in the art of the bail-out, prepared to abandon ship, only to find his trousers were completely stuck to the tar and he was about to be dragged down into the icy depths.

A bit of quick thinking got him out of that scrape. The town of Skerrils will not soon forget the sight of Steven striding smartly up Main Street, drookit, in his underpants, a focused expression on his face as he planned his next attempt at the island.

Vicky

Anyway, while Callum is shaking his head at Steven's silliness and wondering whether Vicky will be more help, there is a certain quick green figure dancing unseen over the kelp and thrift behind him. Or is it in front of him? In fact, it's very hard to tell because this mysterious creature seems able to pop up in one place, vanish, and appear somewhere else seconds later.

If you were watching it, you might say it was dancing—it certainly twirls around a lot, and it seems to hop and skip and stand on its hands—but if it *is* a dance, it's a very weird one. It's more as if it's tummelling, or swaying, or moving with the breeze; it almost rolls in upon itself, shifting shape like clouds in a summer sky.

Somehow, in amongst this strange clamjamfry, the green thing gives the strong impression that it is very interested in Callum. It's not so much following him as surrounding him, and there might just be a sense of *impatience* coming from it. Is it wanting to be *noticed*?

If it is, it's disappointed. Callum doesn't notice the thing at all. No, he's too wrapped up in his own thoughts (and, to be fair, too busy trying to get the smell of clarty cow-corpse out his nostrils) to notice anything much. He's climbed over the harbour wall and is now heading up Seaview Road. But this green apparition will not be ignored for long. With one last ruffle of its leaf-like limbs, it dives head first into the ground and vanishes. Callum spins round and looks for an instant, as if he's finally realised strange things are afoot, but he's quickly distracted by the swift kick up the backside that is Vicky's usual form of greeting.

"Where've you been?" she asks as Callum spins around. Vicky's not one to waste time on 'hellos'.

Callum grins. "Och, just trying to stop Steven from killing himself. What are you up to?"

Vicky falls into step with him, and they move up Seaview Road, a dingy wee street that leads from the harbour up to the main street.

"Learning this," she replies, pulling a recorder out of her inside jacket pocket. Vicky is as naturally musical as a songbird. In fact, she's always reminded Callum of a robin, the way she just pops up with her keen, dark eyes, enjoys your company but always seems seconds away from disappearing on some other errand. (Her usual outfit of a red T-shirt and brown jeans does add to the impression.) And the music—it's ridiculous, really. She understands instruments the way other people understand speech.

"Any luck?" asks Callum.

Vicky shrugs, puts the recorder to her lips, and out skirls a perfect series of reels and jigs, grace notes skipping off the melody like sunlight glinting off water.

The music, as always, makes Callum grin, and he can't help jigging away in time. Passers-by turn their heads, and an elderly couple pause to hear the performance with approving smiles. A mum with a baby in a papoose jounces the wee fellow to the rhythm, making him squeal in delight. Only the minister, a dreich old soul called Mr. MacQuarrie, scowls as he passes, and that's because it's Sunday and he doesn't like seeing folk enjoying themselves. He stalks off, shaking his grey head and chuntering grumpily like a rusty old bicycle.

Callum and the rest of the passing audience applaud when Vicky's finished. "That was great," he says. "When did you get yourself a recorder?"

"Yesterday afternoon." Vicky looks at the instrument as if it's no longer terribly interesting. "Do you want it?"

Callum's about as musical as a box of angry seagulls, but he remembers that Papa used to play a bit so he accepts it happily.

"So, do you still think you blew up the school?" asks Vicky as they carry on up past the library. Callum, pausing briefly to wave in the window to Miss Duguid, the librarian, answers thoughtfully.

"Well, no, not really. But I think it *did* have something to do with me. Papa was starting to tell me about the writing the other day—you know, the message in Gaelic. But when he tried to explain it properly, he kind of went all quiet, like he couldn't really say much. It was weird, like he'd lost his voice or something. I said he could tell me about it later, and he just nodded, and started talking about trout fishing instead!"

Vicky is listening, though it's hard to tell. She keeps skipping ahead a step, twirling round to look backwards, and drumming her fingers on her thighs in time with some internal tune. If you didn't know her, you would probably find all this a bit rude, or at least terribly distracting, but luckily Callum has known Vicky since they were both babies, and he knows that, for her at least, this is perfectly normal behaviour.

"Mmm-hmm," she responds helpfully.

"Anyway," says Callum, "I don't suppose it really matters. Unless other things start blowing up around me, of course."

"Well, stay away from my house until you're sure."

Callum can't tell whether or not she's joking. They're passing the charity shop now, and before he can answer, she's said a cheerful "Bye, then!" and dived inside to look for some new instrument to conquer.

"Aye, cheerio," says Callum to himself, half annoyed, half laughing. Off she flies, as usual.

So, by now, he's made his way past the swing park, where Steven's little brother Harry is playing 'Trog Touch' with some pals—this is a version of 'tig' which involves slapping imaginary fleas off each other's backs—and he's headed towards Papa's house. He feels the weight of the recorder in his pocket so decides he may as well drop by. Up the wee street he goes, feeling suddenly cool in the shade of the rickety old cottages although the sun's bleezin down from a cloudless blue and the ageless mountain is shimmering in the heat-haze above the town. At last he's standing outside Papa's house and is about to push the door open when he hears voices, coming from inside.

"You'll never understand us, will you?" It's Papa's voice, and for one confused moment, Callum thinks he's talking to *him*, though he doesn't see how Papa can know he's there. In a second, though, there's a reply, and oh! It's a strange sound. It *is* a voice, but it sounds more like a wind blowing through leaves, and it sends a chill down Callum's spine. There are words, but they're not in English; they sound more like the Gaelic Papa sometimes mutters in. Callum's frozen to the spot.

"He's just a wee laddie!" Papa's voice again, gruff and maybe a wee bit anxious. Then there's the weird *shooshing*, whispering voice, and Callum can almost smell the leaves and needles of the Old Wood in the sound.

Papa gives an impatient snort. "Well, if you'll not let me help him, you'll maybe have a long wait. He'll maybe never *twig,* if you'll pardon the pun! Weans are different now, you know—not like when *we* first met!"

There's a pause, a silence, then Papa carries on.

"I suppose it would be too much to ask that you just go and *introduce yourself* to him?"

At this, the whooshing, brattling, reeshling sound becomes laughter, rattling the windowpanes and bursting past Callum on its way out the door, and as he staggers backwards, he thinks he hears it whistling off, down the lane, off up the green hill past the monument and beyond.

Papa's door swings open in its wake, and Callum, bumbaiselt, steps inside.

Max

Now, by this time *you*, being the clever person you are, know perfectly well that this scurrilous, perilous, whispering green beastie is the cause of Callum's confusion. You'll also have guessed that Papa's mixed up in all this somehow, and you may well be hoping that he's going to help poor Callum figure out the mystery.

Well, I'm afraid you're about to be disappointed, because it is the nature of the strange green thing and all creatures like it that you cannot be *told* about them and believe it. You have to, absolutely *have* to, see them for yourself. Once you have seen them, life's never the same again and your days on Planet Earth suddenly make both a whole lot more and whole lot less sense at the same time.

The thing you'll want to do more than *anything* is tell everyone you know about your incredible discovery, and you will try—you'll puggle yourself in the trying, in fact—and you will be deeply and profoundly maddened by the fact that no-one else seems to see them. So spare a thought for poor Papa here, because he's known these beings for decades, and he wouldn't be who he is without the things they've taught him, but he is a victim of their peculiar magic in that he cannot give one word of explanation to his favourite grandson.

And look, here's Callum, standing in front of him, hands on hips, accusing.

"Who were you talking to just there, Papa?" he demands.

Papa clenches his jaws and gives a ghastly grin. He opens his mouth as if to speak, but nothing comes out.

"Is this something to do with the school blowing up?" Callum persists.

Papa's mouth opens and closes like a goldfish's, and he sits himself up straight in his armchair. His brow is furrowed, and he looks as if he's making a tremendous effort. With a cough and a splutter, he finally manages to say something.

"Nice weather we're having, isn't it?" he spits through gritted teeth before thumping the arm of his chair in obvious frustration.

Now, Callum's not blind, and he realises there's something amiss. His questions disappear in his concern for his Papa and he's down on his knees beside him, patting him on the back.

"Papa! It's okay!" he says as the old man slowly slumps back in the chair, peching and panting. "What's wrong? Are you all right?" And almost as alarming as

Papa's discomfort is the fact that as soon as the subject has changed, he is immediately absolutely fine again. He sits up straight and looks at Callum with a big smile.

"Fine, son, fine," he says. "Good to see you. What brings you here?"

Callum's a bit startled, as you might well imagine, but kind lad that he is, he swallows down his frustration and decides not to force the subject.

"Em, here." He reaches into his pocket for the recorder. "I brought you this. I thought you might like to play it!" He hands it over, and Papa, delighted, gives it a wee tootle straight away.

"Och here, that's great, laddie. I've not had one of these in years. Will you have a cup of tea?"

Usually, this would be Callum's cue to take a seat and settle in for a pleasant afternoon of blethering, but just at the moment, he gets the feeling that the only thing he wants to talk about is the one thing that he *can't* talk about, so he makes his excuses and politely leaves.

So now it's more obvious than ever that something strange is going on, and Callum is more than a wee bit creeped out. Even as he steps out of Papa's front door, he has a brief feeling that he's being watched, like something's keeking at him from behind some hidden realm. He looks nervously over his shoulder but, of course, there's nothing to see. That would be *far* too easy.

"I need to clear my head," he says to himself. It's still a beautiful day, so he decides to walk up to the monument to see if Craig is there.

Craig is pretty much the only person in Skerrils with a smartphone. They're basically useless in the town because there's no reception, but that didn't stop Craig's parents buying him one. Craig's parents buy him lots and lots of things, and Callum is sometimes a little envious except that buying things seems to be the only thing they do for Craig. They never take him anywhere, barely talk to him at home, and often seem to wish he wasn't there at all.

Craig, adaptable lad that he is, often *decides* not to be there. On his wanderings, he has discovered that the hilltop with the war memorial on it actually *does* get mobile reception, so he takes his phone up there to play video games with cyber-buddies around the world. Aye, up on that peaceful hilltop, under the mountain's silent gaze, Craig has slaughtered his way through many a digital army: zombies, aliens, gladiators...he's massacred them all. Once in a while, Callum likes to join him, the excitement of the games making up for the fact that Craig can be rather sulky company sometimes. So off Callum goes, heading to the gate into Farmer McKenzie's field and the path up the hill, when who should step in his way but Max.

"I hear you're saying you blew up the school, Callum," he squeaks. Max likes to think he's a big man in town. Since nearly everyone leaves Skerrils as soon as they're old enough, there's a serious lack of misplaced youth in the town, so even a fourteen-year-old like Max can pretend to be a tough guy. Sadly for him, his voice is still breaking, and it squeaks and grunts as he issues his blood-curdling threats and no-one takes him terribly seriously. Still, he is bigger than Callum, and if he gets you alone he can get a bit physical, so Callum's far from delighted to see him.

Callum takes a deep breath. "Em, no, not really," he says. He tries to step past Max and carry on under the cool hawthorns and up through the field, but big, tough Max steps in his path and blocks his way.

"Good!" he says in his raspy wee voice. "You'd better not be saying that, because it was *me* that done it and *you're* not getting the credit!"

Now, squeaky and scraichy though Max's voice is, there's an undeniable threat in it, but just for today, Callum's really not in the mood.

"Och, Max," he says with a boldness that comes of impatience and frustration, "stop talking out your backside!"

Can you imagine how mad this makes Max? Being spoken to like this by a twelve-year-old? He draws himself up to his full height—about an inch taller than Callum—and bellows, "What did you just say to me?"

But oh, my goodness me. The voice does not issue from his quivering lips.

No. As a sudden wind comes tremmling through the hawthorns, Max's angry enquiry comes tooting directly out his bahoukie. His face, usually bright red, goes suddenly pale, and Callum nearly falls down at the shock of it.

"Wh...what's happening?" Max's voice is suddenly tiny, frightened, but it's still not coming from his mouth. It's coming muffled through the seat of his trousers. "This is impossible!" squeaks his tearful posterior, and as Callum's head spins with the bizarre impossibility of it all, Max turns and flees, a final "*Heeeellllllppppp!*" escaping from his fleggit backside.

Callum, at least as scared and bewildered as Max, turns, leaps over the yett, and flees up to the monument to find Craig...

...leaving in his wake, by the way, a number of cackling, rolling figures, wheezing with mirth on the fringe of reality, just beyond anywhere that Callum can yet see, among them our strange and irksome quick green friend of before.

Craig

Hell for leather, Callum's away, sprinting up the rocky path, through the field, dodging round the whin bushes and scattering rabbits and pheasants as he goes.

"*Craiiiig!*" he bellows as the monument bobs into sight. "CRAIIIIIG!"

A short, dark-haired figure sitting with his back against the sunny side of the monument glances up at the frantic sight of Callum, but apparently it's not enough to keep his attention from something he's holding in his hand. He looks back down as Callum, breathless and sweating, arrives at his side.

"*CraigyouarenotgoingtoBELIEVEwhatjusthappened IwastalkingtoMaxandhisvoicestartedcoming out ofhis...*" jabbers Callum, his face red and his arms waving around like a disco dancer's.

"*Shoosh!*" snaps Craig, his eyes focused on the smartphone in his hands. "You're putting me off!"

Callum stops abruptly, taking the chance to catch his breath, the thudding in his ears slowly giving way to the bleeps, explosions and mortal screams coming from

Craig's device. The sound effects mix oddly with the cry of distant gulls, and the trilling warble of a skylark high in the blue. Callum's not to be discouraged for long. He draws in a long breath.

"*CRAIG!*" he bellows, making his friend jump. This reaction is followed by some tinny, doom-laden music, and Craig looks up furiously.

"Callum, I was *just* about to reach level five and you've *gone and got me killed!*" Callum gives a snort of impatience.

"Forget about your stupit Call of Warfare or whatever the heck it is. This is *important*!"

"It's *Call of Duty*, you idiot, and *it's* important! I've been trying to crack that level for an hour and a half!" Craig is all set to turn his attention back to the game, but Callum gets down to eye level with a don't-ignore-me-this-is-serious expression on his face.

"Listen, Craig, *very weird things are happening!* I've just heard Max *talking out of his BUM*!"

Craig looks confused. "That's what he always does, isn't it?" he asks.

"No, I mean REALLY talking out his bum! He's terrified! I've no idea how it happened, but I swear, his voice was coming from—"

"Yeah, yeah, yeah, very funny," says Craig, now looking with determination back at his phone. He's swiped his finger across the screen and the music and explosions have started again. Craig stabs at the screen and eruptions of gunfire can be heard from its little speakers. "*Yes!*" he exclaims, having presumably just slaughtered his way through a crowd of enemy combatants.

Callum stands up. He's furious. Why won't anyone take him seriously? Breathing deeply, he glances at the monument, a granite obelisk carved with the names of Skerrils men lost in the World Wars. *They'd* believe him. They wouldn't waste their time playing games when there's important business about. There are Campbells, Maxwells, MacQuarries and MacArthurs—more names than you'd expect from a wee place like Skerrils. It's not the first time Callum's read them: black names shining solemnly from the smooth grey stone.

Callum frames his next statement carefully, trying to think of the words that will convince Craig there is something going on in the *real* world which is *much* more interesting than the electronic bloodshed that has currently grabbed his attention. He paces round the monument, through its needling shadow, and reappears in front of Craig. *Right. Here goes.*

But before he can say anything, he is thrown onto his back in gaping consternation as the smooth, flat surface of the monument suddenly forms itself into a malevolent, mislushious, grinning *face*. Great stone eyes skinkle down at him as the black unchancy hole of the face's mouth opens itself wide.

"*Crr...Crai...C...C...*" stammers Callum in a gasp and a whisper.

"Wheesht," mutters Craig, intent on throwing a grenade into an enemy bunker. Callum is skittling backwards on his elbows like a startled crab, too astonished to mind the thistles and whin, as the great, grinning monolith bends itself over Craig. Its shining point is now looming right over him, blocking out the sun, and Craig is at last distracted by the sudden shade. He glances over his shoulder in surprise, just in time to see a muckle, gaping mouth of stone bearing down on him.

"*OH, MY, G—*" he yells, but his cry is snuffed like a candle as the grinning granite lips smack themselves closed around him. The ground rumbles with the sound of a monolithic *gulp,* the monument grins wickedly at Callum, winks, gives itself a shoogle and then, as quick as blinking, everything is completely normal again.

Craig's phone beeps and chirps to itself abandoned on the grass, the skylark is still singing, and Callum's mouth is open in a silent scream.

Seconds later, he is bounding back down the hillside, crashing through undergrowth, and yelling for help like a boy demented.

Things-of-Green

Here he goes, look, hurtling down through the green field towards the town below, beyond it the great silver sea like a glittering shawl around Skerrils' stony shoulders. Callum's approaching the gate and preparing to take it in a single leap (he's managed it once before with a lot less motivation) when he sees Vicky opening it and heading through. She's carrying something nearly as big as herself, and if Callum doesn't take evasive action, he's going to crash right into her.

With a whoop of fright, he tries to stop his pounding feet, and his arms windmill around as he desperately attempts to check his thundering momentum. Predictably enough, poor Callum loses control completely; his left foot hits a hawthorn root, and he catapults forward, heelster-gowdie-clattering down in a dishevelled, thorn-torn, muddy bloody heap at Vicky's feet. A cloud of dust rises gently as he lands, and the world carousels around his poor dunted head.

"Oh, hi," says Vicky.

Callum sits up, gasping and wheezing in his stoory cloud. He has briefly forgotten what it was he was running from, and his senses are kept busy by trying to make sense of what Vicky is carrying.

"Is...is that a *cello*?" he asks as he climbs painfully to his feet.

Vicky grins, her dark eyes sparkling. "It sure is," she says. She seems to have no interest at all in Callum's unusual arrival at her feet. "Check this out! It was only seven quid!" She strokes the strings lovingly and draws the bow expertly across them, calling forth a deep, mellow scale which ends in a shimmering vibrato. "I'm away up to the monument to practise!"

Suddenly everything floods back into Callum's mind and he grabs Vicky's shoulders in alarm.

"No!" he yells. "You *can't* go up there! The thing's *alive*! I've just seen it swallow Craig!"

Vicky shakes herself free from Callum's grasp and steps back, shielding her precious cello and pointing the bow at him in warning.

"Very funny, "she says. "No, really, hilarious. You know, Callum, your stories are getting a bit..." She pauses as she searches for a word, but being Vicky, she quickly loses her train of thought and makes to head on up the path without finishing her sentence.

Callum, bruised and frightened, steps in her way. "Vicky, you *can't*! You can't just flit away this time. This is *serious*! Very, very weird things are happening!"

"Weird things are *always* happening in your head, Callum," says Vicky, not without a wee touch of affection, "but I'm busy just now. I'm... I've got to... That is..." A very peculiar expression appears on Vicky's face, and her dark eyes turn on Callum with a look of baffled anxiety. Callum feels a deep, dark dread as he realises something is wrong, and going on recent experience, that could mean just about anything.

"What is it? Vicky, what's the matter?" he demands, as Vicky, in an oddly hypnotised fashion, carefully lays the cello on the ground and places the bow beside it. She stands, turns to face Callum again with that same look of doitit confusion on her face. A sudden snell wind ruffles the grass, a solitary cloud passes over the sun, Vicky gives a kind of shudder and then, before Callum's startled eyes, she gently folds and tumbles in on herself as brown and red feathers pop sleekly through her skin. In an instant—so quickly, in fact, that Callum can barely register the transition—there is a merry wee robin hopping and pecking around where Vicky had been standing not two seconds before.

"Vicky!" shrieks Callum, clasping his head in his hands in shock. "Vicky!" The robin startles into the air for a second, lands on the scroll of the cello, casts him an accusing look and then flits off through the hawthorns and into the shadows. A peal of bittersweet, liquid birdsong issues through the green leaves, and Vicky is gone.

Callum reels. *It's a prank—it has to be. It's some kind of conjuring trick. There'll be some smart-alec with a camera hiding in the trees.* Or else he's hallucinating. Maybe he caught a fever from Steven's rotting cow and he's having delirious visions.

But he knows it's not so. Something is turning his world upside down. There has to be some kind of reason for this.

"It's NOT FUNNY!" he yells into the sky, and the cloud rolls away from the sun, chasing its shadow off up the distant mountain and briefly blinding him in the flood of sunlight.

But there's a baffling green being who thinks that, in fact, it is, very, very funny indeed, and it's not quite ready to let Callum off the hook yet. It's right next to him, you know, but it's not letting itself be seen. It skips delightedly out of the way as Callum, jaw set in grim determination, marches off in search of Steven and his last hope of being believed.

On through the streets of Skerrils he strides, ignoring the greetings of the people he passes, muttering and mithering under his breath. He doesn't even cross the street to avoid the scowling Mr. MacQuarrie, as he would usually do, merely stalking past him and ignoring the little cloud of gloom the minister carries around with him.

Callum doesn't stop till he gets to the harbour wall, which he vaults up onto, stamps along, and leaps off onto the shingle shore beyond. On he clatters, round the coast to Steven's workshop, burning with the knowledge that nothing's going to stop him getting to the bottom of this impenetrable weirdness; nothing can distract him from his quest.

Nothing, that is, but the frankly unbelievable sight of Steven cheerfully rowing a makeshift boat halfway out to MacArthur's Island and apparently, stunningly, not sinking.

"Ahoy there!" yells Steven. "Hey, Callum! Look at me!" He stands up in the boat, which looks as if it might once have been the roof of a shed, and waves his paddle about triumphantly. "What do you think of *this*?"

Callum, astonished, lets out a gasp of laughter. "Where did you find *that*?" he bellows across the water.

But Steven's answer is lost in a sudden surge of rushing water, a bubbling, gurgling, splashing cacophony, as the sea between the two friends is gripped in a boiling torment. Steven falls backwards and disappears briefly in the bowels of his boat, and Callum leaps away from the waterline in shock.

A huge, dark shape is forming itself beneath the once-calm waters of the bay. At first Callum thinks it must be the shadow of a cloud, but one glance up into the blue tells him it's not so. No—there's something down there.

The shape gets bigger and blacker as the thing, whatever it is, rises from the depths. Steven has reappeared and his hands are gripping the sides of the rocking, bouncing boat so hard that his knuckles have gone white.

"WHALE!" he shrieks, as rolling surges of foamy water threaten to swamp his flimsy wee vessel. The shape keeps growing until at last a vast, smooth, black surface breaks the sea and rises. It is peppered with barnacles, hung with seaweed, shining wetly in the startled sunlight, and Callum reckons that Steven is right. It must be a whale! Amazing! There's never, *ever* been a whale seen in the bay before!

But oh, great heavens above, it's no whale in the bay right now! For up ahead of this sleek, black back, a sinuous, serpentine neck bursts forth, shedding torrents of water into the bubbling brine below. At its tip, a grinning reptilian head leers down from the sky, and hungry, golden eyes glare at Callum before it snakes around towards Steven. With a thrash of its twisting tail, the monster is upon him, pushing forward a bow wave so powerful it lifts both Steven and his boat clean out of the water. The boat falls back into the waves and collapses, quickly disappearing beneath the surface and spiralling down to join all of Steven's previous efforts in the murky depths below.

Steven, though, has no such escape. With its dripping, hungry jaws, the monster snatches him out of the sky, tips its head back and swallows him down before plunging off into the hidden depths with only a trail of disappearing foam to show where it has been.

And all of a sudden, whether our troublesome green friend wants it or not, Callum can see him, clear as day, as he rolls and cackles on the tideline. Human-shaped but far from human, it is flailing and hooting like storm-tossed treetops, a weird confusion of twiggish limbs and skinkling, glinting, green eyes.

"You! It's *you!*" bellows Callum, and it's as if he's always known this pestering, mischievous, green rapscallion, has felt its presence his whole life. He strides over the pebbles towards it with a wrathful glare, and for once, the sleekit green beastie is alarmed. It leaps to its feet and tries to backflip away from the furious Callum but is too slow.

Callum *leaps* at it and grasps it by its fluttering green shoulders, and now he's *shaking* the thing, shoogling and rattling it till its teeth—if it *has* teeth—must be clacking in its bothersome green head.

"*GIVE—ME—BACK—MY—FRIENDS!*"   yells Callum as he shakes and worries at the apparition before him.

But this beast is not *quite* so easily cowed. It reaches up one twiggish, rustling hand and taps Callum on the forehead, whereupon he freezes like a statue, allowing the creature to step calmly out of his way.

"We are Things-of-Green," it whispers in a strange and lilting voice, "and we will return your friends when we are good and ready!" And with that, it claps its hands and is gone.

Missing

Whether it is shock, horror, or the mischievous magic of Things-of-Green, minutes go by and poor Callum still cannot move. He is glued to the spot like a tattie-bogle, his ginger fringe ruffled by the breeze as the baffling normality of the world surges in around him. It's just a sunny day on a shingle beach in the West of Bonnie Scotland. The sea's lapping sweetly at the shore, a busy scatter of plovers are probing around in the tideline, and there's the occasional rumble of a car coming into town. Against the ageless backdrop of the mountain, everything is entirely usual...

...except that all of Callum's best friends have just been torn from him in the most terrifying ways imaginable, and it seems as if some sort of bizarre nature spirit is responsible. It is quite a lot for a twelve-year-old to take in. He wishes he could tell his friends about it, but then he realises that, *oh yes*, they already know.

So he's standing there in a total dwam until he feels the warmth of a gentle hand on his shoulder, and without even looking, he knows it's Papa. When the familiar, rumbling voice comes, it's as much a part of the landscape as the cry of the gulls or the outline of the island in the hazy distance.

"How are you feeling, laddie?" asks Papa quietly.

At once, of course, the spell is broken and everything floods over poor Callum. He folds himself into his Papa's arms and bursts into vigorous, snottery tears. Papa pats his back and gives him a squeeze.

"Here, now, Callum, it's okay, it's okay." He breaks the embrace but keeps his hands on his grandson's shoulders.

Callum looks up at him through bloodshot eyes, gives a shudder and draws his sleeve briskly across his face with a snuffle. He doesn't like to cry in front of Papa, so with an effort he pulls himself together and even manages a watery smile. Papa waits, patiently.

"Sorry," says Callum, but Papa just smiles.

"Come on, laddie," he says, and a couple of minutes later, they are sitting on a broad wooden bench overlooking the bay, which has been pleasantly warmed in the sun.

Now, it has to be said that although Callum is very grateful for Papa's company—and actually, when he comes to think of it, pretty astonished to see Papa out of doors—he's not all that optimistic about the conversation they're going to have. After all, he's tried asking about this already, and all it seems to do is turn Papa into a gibbering wreck.

Callum cannot help but feel he has enough to worry about at the moment without having to carry a stottering octogenarian back to his cottage. So you can just about imagine his surprise when Papa, pipe lit and comfortable, turns to him and says, "So, you'll have met Things-of-Green now, I take it?"

Callum's look of astonishment draws a deep, throaty chuckle from Papa.

"You...you *know* it, then?" gasps Callum. "I *knew* you knew something about it! Why didn't you *tell* me when I asked you?" There's more confusion than anger in the question, and Papa sooks thoughtfully at his pipe.

"Well, now, you see, laddie," he says carefully, "these friends of ours are complicated creatures. You can't just go around blethering about them to anyone who'll listen. You see..." He's settling in for a long explanation, but Callum has to object.

"*Friends?*" he yelps. "That *thing*, whatever it is, isn't my *friend*! It's too busy *eating* my friends and turning them into birds to be one itself!" The emotion is rising in Callum's voice, and he stands up to pace back and forth. "Papa, *all my friends* are missing! What am I going to do? Should I go to the police?"

Papa gives a short, choking cough which sends a merry plume of blue smoke up into the atmosphere.

"Oh, dear me, no, Callum," he chuckles. "There's precisely nothing the police can do. And, you know, it's hard for you to see it, but these things *are* your friends. If you *let* them be, that is. Come here, look."

He pats the bench beside him and Callum sits back down, curiosity getting the better of his anger.

"Now," says Papa, "I want you to look around you. But *really* look. Look at the grass. Look at the trees. Take a look at the seaweed and the shingle, look at the water. *Look* at it all, Callum, and tell me what's changed."

It takes a minute for Callum to settle down enough to do what he's told, but at last he takes a deep breath and casts his eye at the scene around him. At first, he doesn't notice anything unusual; Callum's always been an observant lad, and he *knows* what a beautiful spot he lives in. So, yes, there's the lovely bay, and the nice green grass, and the trembling leaves of the alder trees by the roadside, sure, and the sea's nice and shimmery and calm, and the sky's all blue, and, and, and...

And suddenly, without warning, Callum is almost knocked backwards by the dazzling realisation that as he looks at this beautiful, glittering scene, the beautiful, glittering scene is *looking right back at him*. Everything is looking at him, watching him with warm regard. Each bouncing blade of grass, every wave that strokes the shore, every centuries-smoothed pebble, every wispy, drifting cloud in the bright blue sky and the gulls that rise and fall with the gentle swell of the sea.

All of them...everything is watching him patiently, expectantly, and from the very centre of his being comes a hoot of delighted laughter as he fills to the brim with a boiling, bubbling, baffling sense of *belonging*. He leaps back to his feet in unfettered delight, spreads his arms wide and laughs aloud again.

And somewhere in the midst of it all, he can sense Steven, and Craig, and Vicky, and he knows they are perfectly safe, knows they are discovering the same thing as him and they'll be reunited soon. Everything is connected, everything is woven together, and Callum grabs Papa in a hug of sheer joy.

"Ah-*ha*," laughs the old man from the midst of this boisterous embrace, "you can see now, can't you!" Callum's rocking laughter is his only reply, and Papa continues with a chuckle in his voice. "This is *them*, you understand, laddie?"

Callum releases his Papa and sits back, his face split by an enormous grin. "Yes, I do! I really do! But how do they do it, Papa?"

Papa shrugs. "Not the foggiest, I'm afraid!"

"What are they?" asks Callum.

"Don't know!"

"How many of them are there?"

"Don't ask me!"

You might well think this would be a bit of a frustrating conversation, and if it had taken place ten minutes ago, Callum would have thought so too. But now, seeing what he sees, it fills him with delight and excitement at the glorious mystery of things. He takes a deep, delicious breath and looks again at the scene, and in amongst all the shimmering interest of the natural world, he gets a sense of Things-of-Green. It's as if he can *feel* him, even though he's not right there; he can effortlessly call him to mind, him and a whole crowd of others like him, all waiting in the wings for the next merry dance. It is wonderful, hilarious, full of fizzing excitement.

But there's something else there too. Almost... almost a *sadness?*

Callum's thoughts are interrupted by Papa. "What I *can* tell you," says the old man, "is that they don't show themselves to just anybody. They have to *like* you!"

Well, they chat for a wee bit longer, Papa suggesting that Callum take a look in the 'folklore' section of the library—"These things have been known in these parts for as long as people have lived here—see if you can find them in the old stories!"

Eventually, Callum senses that Papa is growing tired, and at last they get up to wander back through the town and home. They're walking up Main Street, slowly, as Papa hirples along on his gammy leg, when suddenly something occurs to Callum.

"Papa, won't my friends be missed? I mean, what am I going to tell Vicky's folks? And Steven's, and Craig's? What if they don't come back?"

Papa pauses, pulls a big silk hankie out of his pocket to dab his brow and catches his breath.

"Callum," he says, "in 1953, my sweetheart Elsa, who was to become your granny, took a stroll in the woods and vanished. Things-of-Green had decided he liked her and wanted to show her the other land, the place where he and the others seem to spend most of their time. No, no, no questions just now, laddie." He waves away the enquiry he sees forming on Callum's lips. "Now, Elsa was gone a whole year. No word, no sign, no trace. A whole year, mind." Papa gives a shudder at what is clearly not a very pleasant memory. He shakes his head in disbelief. "Do you know how many people went looking for her? How many people asked about her?"

"How many?" asks Callum breathlessly.

"None." Papa has a distant look in his eyes. He shakes his head again and laughs. "Look, I'll show you." They happen to be near Steven's house, so Papa takes Callum's hand and leads him to it, opens the gate and heads up the path. "Chap the door," he says, and Callum does so.

"Round here!" shouts a voice from the back garden, so Callum and Papa make their way up the side passage and through the rickety wooden gate. In the garden, they find Steven's dad Michael, standing with his hands on his hips and staring at his garden shed with a look of deep perplexity. Understandably, since the shed is missing its entire roof and is standing, topless, in a delicate pile of sawdust.

"Look at this!" he says to Callum and Papa without wasting any time on hellos. "Look what some wee toerag's done to my blinking shed!"

Callum suddenly realises where Steven acquired his last boat from, but of course, he doesn't want to get his friend into trouble. To his surprise, though, Papa nudges him and gives him an encouraging nod.

"Tell him, Callum," he says.

Now remember, Callum's still filled with the weird warm glow of his recent experiences, so he gives a what-the-heck kind of a shrug and says, "Mr. Campbell, I think Steven did that to make himself a boat."

Steven's dad looks at Callum. There's a blank expression on his face.

"Who's Steven?" he asks.

"Och, nobody, Michael," says Papa. "Callum's in a bit of a dwam today. Sorry to bother you!" And he leads Callum back out up the street, chuckling all the way.

Dream

That night, Callum is tucked up in his cosy bed, Mum and Dad downstairs watching the telly, when the great, gazing cosmos creeps into his dreaming mind. He finds himself standing on an impossibly green hillside with the whole wide mindful world around him. Oceans and lochs glitter under an azure sky, and the sun is a humming, singing, burning ball in the sky.

"*Failte*," says a voice behind him, and he turns to see Things-of-Green standing there. But this is not the strange, shimmery leaf-creature he met on the beach. Things-of-Green is tall, majestic and obviously ancient. If he had seemed a mischievous dandelion type before, here, he is nothing short of a grand old oak, and Callum is at once impressed and a little scared. There's nothing of the flightiness of before, either; Things-of-Green seems decidedly rooted to the spot, drawing power from the ground and casting a long, cool shadow. He speaks again.

"Welcome, Callum Maxwell," he says, and his voice is deep and powerful. "You have been a long time coming."

Callum's not sure what to say.

"Ehm... Sorry?" he tries, and immediately feels silly.

The figure before him ignores this completely, merely fixing Callum with a penetrating gaze. Callum feels all the power of the landscape, all the energy and focus he felt on the beach with Papa, beaming directly at him from those strange, dark eyes. He is mesmerised.

After a while, he becomes aware that it is growing dark. The sun is sinking rapidly below the horizon and stars have begun to wheel above in the darkening blue. Callum realises there are more beings behind him, and without turning round he is suddenly able to see them. They are tall and terrible like Things-of-Green, but different too, each one bathed in its own strange smeddum.

One is pitted and scarred like the sea cliffs round the bay, chiselled, solid, dangerous. *We are Things-of-Stone,* it seems to say.

Another glitters and moves, crystalline like ice yet ever changing as the clouds. *Things-of-Water are we,* it tells him, somehow, deep in his mind.

Another is clawed, feathered, furred and fierce. Its scales glance in the starlight, and its eyes shine and pulse in a steady, beating rhythm. *Things-of-Blood, Callum Maxwell,* it tells him.

There are others, more mysterious and more distant, each of them ancient, still and strong, surrounding him like the standing stones at the Holy Cairn. Callum is suddenly overwhelmed with memories, from his earliest recollection of gazing at the sky from his pram as a baby, to his first jaunts in the hills with his dad; swimming in the sea on cool spring days, the sudden delicious shock of the water; sitting, perfectly hidden, in his treehouse, safe and superior.

These beings, these entities, have been there all along, watching, observing, holding it all together somehow, and Callum cannot understand how it is that he hasn't realised this before.

A robin alights at his feet, gives a burst of sharp, clear song and stretches itself blissfully back into Vicky. Things-of-Stone leans forward solemnly, opens its giant, rocky hand, and out leaps Craig, dusting himself down and grinning. Things-of-Water and Things-of-Blood turn to face each other, join their mighty hands, and lower Steven down as if from the clouds above. He lands on the grass with a bounce and a roll, gets up and steps towards his friends. They are reunited and they don't need to say a word; one look at each other shows they all *know*.

"We are glad you are here," comes a voice—maybe from one of the creatures, maybe from all of them at once. "We are glad you could come. It is *necessary*."

"What do you mean?" asks Callum. He feels no fear now, only an urgent curiosity, a desire to understand more fully. "What do you want from us?"

"Much," comes the reply as the strange, towering figures rise around him. "We have need of you, children."

Callum, Vicky, Craig and Steven look at each other with a thrill of wonder.

"*YOU* have need of *US*?" says Vicky. "But you... you're all so *powerful*!"

The others nod; they have felt this too, the sense that these creatures have all the great, grinding power of nature in their very fingertips. What help can four wee kids from Skerrils possibly give them?

"That," says Things-of-Green, "will become clear in time. First, though, since we have your attention..." He claps his hands, and suddenly he is once again the quick, fluttering creature of twig and leaf, the laughing, pliskie sprite who has danced Callum into all this mischief. Around him, his fellows have made similar transformations, zipping down to child-size, no bigger than Callum and his friends, and they dance and spin and cackle around them with the energy of an April storm.

"Now we have your *attention*," repeats Things-of-Green in his rustling whisper, "perhaps we should have some *fun*!"

Each of the children is suddenly grabbed by one of the dancing, skirling creatures and *flung* off the hillside, hurtling through the yawning blue and over the edge of a giddying cliff. Wind howls in their ears, and they open their mouths and yell as cruel, wave-beaten rocks rush up to meet them and *BANG!*

They are all four sitting in their pyjamas on the lawn in Callum's back garden. The grass is wet with dew—and so are their pyjamas—and they can only stare at each other in open-mouthed befuddlement. Through their confusion, they realise it is morning, and all four of them jump at the sound of Callum's back door opening.

"Here, you four," says Callum's mum, "do you want some breakfast or not?"

Part 2

Dog

So the sun rises merrily on another glorious summer day in Skerrils, and Callum, Vicky, Craig and Steven can't wait to get out and about. They head indoors and find their clothes waiting for them in neat piles in Callum's room, as if they've just enjoyed a normal sleepover. Grinning, they get dressed in double-quick time and charge downstairs to the kitchen to eat.

They have an overwhelming sense of things waiting to happen; huge, enormous, momentous things. As they sit around the breakfast table, they are itching to discuss their recent adventures, each one of them desperate to jabber at length about the strange and terrifying Things-of-Stone, the gloriously devilish Things-of-Green, the weird timeless land which they command as solemn giants and the bizarre adventures which they feel sure will now await them.

The trouble is, though, that in Callum's house, it is customary to sit together at the table for meals, so the four friends are impatiently munching their cornflakes in the company of Callum's mum and dad. This means that, try as they might, they cannot say a single word about their discoveries. Every time, it either comes out as a pointless nonsense like...

"I wish they'd make a film about dinosaurs with helicopters."

...or else it's complete gibberish, like...

"Plufwuffle borgle, borglorium plop!"

This is making for an odd conversation.

"What were you four up to yesterday? We hardly saw you all day!" asks Callum's dad.

"We were digging a tunnel to China," answers Callum, with absolutely no idea why he has said such a silly thing. Oddly, his dad isn't too bothered.

"Oh yes? How far did you get?"

"Maglooflum, smlagleedle badeedle, baglum!" answers Steven confidently before clapping his hands over his mouth in astonishment.

"That's nice," says Callum's mum. "So, what's the plan for today then?"

"We're going to gullum gullum gullum maglinty fifty-seven tennis racquets," explains Vicky, before muttering quietly to herself, "Where the blinking flip did the fifty-seven tennis racquets come from?"

As you can imagine, this quickly becomes tiresome, so the four friends excuse themselves and head out the front door.

"Well, that was just plain weird," says Craig, shaking his head. "What was that all about?"

"It's Things-of-Green," explains Callum. "You can't talk about him to people who haven't seen him. It's the reason Papa couldn't tell me about these creatures before yesterday."

"I suppose that makes sense," says Steven thoughtfully. "Otherwise everyone would know about them, wouldn't they?"

They're making for the path up to the monument because Vicky wants to retrieve her cello and Craig wants his phone, and the gate is coming into view, when suddenly the conversation stops abruptly. All four of them have simultaneously become aware of something very weird, although none of them can quite put their finger on it. Vicky looks at Steven. Steven looks at Craig. Craig looks at Callum. Callum looks at...

And then they realise what it is that's bothering them. It is the fact that although they can each see each other perfectly well, and recognise one another as usual, and they can't see anyone there who isn't one of them, there are now quite clearly five of them.

"Ummm..." says Callum, helpfully. "Are you all seeing this?" All four of his companions nod. "And does anyone, ah, have any sort of explanation at all?" Four heads shake in his direction. Callum, giving up, has a wee seat on the grass and scratches his head. "Right," he mutters. "You're Vicky," he says, pointing at her.

"True," replies Vicky.

"You're Steven."

"I am."

"You're Craig.

"That's me."

"So, you're..." says Callum, and you'd think that would have sorted things out, but the fourth person he looks at is just so blasted familiar—and actually *could* be Vicky, or Craig, or Steven, or indeed Callum himself—that he can't think of a way to identify it as anyone else.

The figure looks at him in a friendly way, while the other three all look at it. It's definitely a child. Well, sort of definitely. Well, actually, no, not at all. It's FAR too old to be a child. And it's definitely not one of the gang of friends, except that, well, it actually sort of definitely *is* one of them. In fact, it's *all* of them. And even while he's looking at it, Callum finds his gaze sort of slipping off it and returning to Vicky, or to Steven or Craig, so that he's never exactly certain whether there's anyone else there at all, but for the fact that there very obviously is.

Suddenly, Craig lets out a cry of understanding.

"You're Things-of-Blood!" he yells, and the figure gives a low bow then stands, grinning at them.

"We are!" it replies, and before their disbelieving eyes, it becomes each one of them in turn, then Papa, then Max, then an oystercatcher, then a seal, an eagle, a worm, a salmon and finally a kind of bowksome, seething mixture of the lot. It does this without really seeming to change, as if all these creatures are part of it all at once, and the four friends have to turn away to keep from feeling giddy.

"Oh, stop it, please!" shouts Vicky, and as soon as she does so, Things-of-Blood appears as a sort-of human, about their size, slender and strong and wearing a cloak made of fur. He's as solid and unchanging as anyone, which is almost as unsettling as his earlier performance.

"You see," mutters Steven, "this is exactly the sort of thing I'm talking about! I mean, if everyone could talk about this guy, if everyone could *see* him—"

"Everyone *can* see us, human," says Things-of-Blood. His voice is oddly soothing, warm and rich, and the four children feel their fears melting easily away. "Everyone sees us all the time. It is not *seeing*, but *noticing* that is the problem. Watch!"

Things-of-Blood points down the path, and the children see Mr. McKendrick stalking towards them, shoulders hunched, his yappy wee dog bouncing and skipping along behind him. Mr. McKendrick's dog is a terrier and a dopily friendly wee beast. It loves leaping up to get clapped, and its tail is always pointing delightedly at the sky, usually wagging fit to shake the glaikit wee beast off its feet.

All the children like the dog—most folk in the town like it—even if it is a bit on the noisy side. Indeed, the only person in the town who really seems to dislike the dog is Mr. McKendrick himself, who spends quite a lot of time red in the face and furious as he bellows at the dog to be quiet. His bellowing is much more unpleasant than the dog's barking, but there are few folk in Skerrils with the nerve to tell him as much.

As you can imagine, then, the children aren't that delighted to see him approaching, especially as they can already hear him hollering, "*Shut it, you stupit dug!*" at his bouncy wee companion.

"Yap, yap, yap," replies the dog, happily.

As they approach, Things-of-Blood takes an easy step into their path, does an odd little pirouette, winks at the children and becomes impossible to see again. Mr. McKendrick is now right on the spot where Things-of-Blood was standing, completely ignoring the four children (much to their relief) and bawling spittily at the dog.

"*See if you dinnae shut it, you stupit wee ratbag, I'm gonny chuck ye aff the cliff!*" he yells.

"Yap, yap, yap!" replies the dog.

"*Shut it!*"

"Yap, yap, yap!"

"SHUUUUUUUUT *IIIIIIIITTTTTTTTTTT!!!*"

Mr. McKendrick's voice is hoarse now, and the children can see the veins throbbing in his sweaty red forehead. Their attention is quickly diverted, however, by the dog's next reply.

"My dear fellow, I'm so *terribly* sorry," it says politely.

Callum's jaw drops, and as he watches, the dog stands up on its hind legs and walks over to Mr. McKendrick. It puts a soothing paw on his hip.

"There, there, now," it says, "don't fret so. I'm just so awfully excited to be out on a walk with you, my dear, *dear* master!"

Callum and his friends collapse in laughter at this ridiculous spectacle, but Mr. McKendrick appears not to have noticed anything unusual.

"Whit are you kids laughing at?" he grumbles.

"Oh, don't mind them, my dear fellow," says the dog sweetly. "Laughter is a wonderful thing, is it not? And they are but young. Oh, the sweet foolishness of youth!" And bizarrely, never once acknowledging that his dog is talking to him, Mr. McKendrick seems to calm down a bit.

"Aye, well," he says gruffly, "just watch yersel's!"

The dog gives a big, approving grin. "Wonderful!" it says in delight. "Now, if I'm not much mistaken, I believe we were off on our peregrinations, were we not, oh, beautiful master!"

And off they go.

"I suppose we shouldn't be that surprised," says Vicky after they have recovered from their helpless laughter. "After all, the whole blinking school exploded and everyone more or less forgot about it in a couple of days!"

"Kind of makes you wonder what else goes on under folks' noses," says Callum, and they carry on to fetch the cello and the phone, nodding friendly hellos to all the rocks, trees, shrubs and creatures they pass along the way.

Library

Well now, a few hours go by, and the friends drift their separate ways, as can happen on these long, languorous summer days. All four of them feel changed, and changed forever, but daily life does get in the way. Vicky has to go and play some tunes at the old folks' home; Steven's got to look after his wee brother while his folks go off to Oban to do some shopping; and Craig, who, on finding his phone, looked at it blankly and then decided to leave it where it was, just wants to wander off on his own for a bit. This leaves Callum at a bit of a loose end, so he decides to follow some advice Papa gave him the day before and go to the local library.

"It's yourself, Callum," smiles Miss Duguid as he pushes open the door and steps into the lovely musty dimness. Callum loves the library because it never changes. Summer or winter, morning or evening, the library is just the library, and Miss Duguid is just Miss Duguid: a nice old lady with a smile for everyone. The shelves are of dark old wood, the window is covered by moth-eaten blinds, and a potted cheese plant in the corner quietly gathers dust.

"Hello, Miss Duguid," says Callum. "I'm looking for some books about, um...well, about strange creatures, I suppose."

Miss Duguid leans forward on her desk and peers at Callum with interest. "Do you mean unusual animals, Callum?"

"Well, no, not really. I'm thinking of creatures which are...well, I mean creatures a bit like..." And for a few minutes, Callum is rather lost in confusion as he realises he can't actually describe what sort of creature Things-of-Green might be. Fortunately, Miss Duguid helps him out.

"Are you thinking of *supernatural* creatures, Callum?" she asks.

Callum grins. "Aye, I suppose so!"

"Let's have a wee look in the folklore section, shall we?"

For the next twenty minutes, Callum and Miss Duguid gather a pile of books, from dusty old leather-bound volumes to bright colourful children's books, about Celtic mythology, folklore, faeries and strangeness. All of this is watched by a pair of old gentlemen seated in the corner, as dusty as some of the books, with newspapers open on their laps but no obvious desire to read them. They are always in the library—Callum's never seen them anywhere else—and he thinks of them as Mr. Tweed and Mr. Corduroy after the old blazers they wear. Quite often they seem to be fast asleep, but today they're watching his progress with kindly interest. They nod at him whenever he glances in their direction; this is clearly the best entertainment they've had in a while.

At last, Callum is satisfied that they have enough, so Miss Duguid retires back behind her desk and Callum settles himself at the table for a good old read. He learns of Tam Lin; he learns of Michael Scott, the Borders Wizard; he learns of banshees and brownies and kelpies and giants. He reads of people put to sleep for a thousand years, or swallowed by mountains and never seen again; of babies stolen and replaced with uggsome creatures that wail for comfort and never grow up.

He reads of the Faery Flag of Dunvegan and the great mysterious armies that marched each time it was flown. He finds, to his surprise, that these weird creatures have parts in stories he already knew: it seems that King Arthur and his knights had dealings with them, that the Lady in the Lake might have been one of them and even Merlin himself could have been part faery.

Callum's imagination is alight with long ages past, with this strange meeting of worlds and the comings and goings of mysterious beings between them.

In fact, he would be getting more and more confident in his knowledge of these beasties, were it not for a persistent and noisy fasherie which breaks through his concentration every time he gets absorbed. It's a kind of wheezing, rasping rattle coming from the corner by the window, where Mr. Tweed and Mr. Corduroy are now dozing. *One of them must be snoring*, thinks Callum to himself, and he tries not to be annoyed. The pleasant old men surely have the right to snooze in the peaceful gloom should they want to.

He's in the midst of a story in which the mysterious faery being could actually be Things-of-Green himself, when this rasping rattle cuts through his consciousness again, breaking the spell completely.

"Oh, for goodness' sake..." he mutters, and glowers over at the elderly gentlemen.

"*Shhhh!*" says Miss Duguid from her desk.

Callum mouths "Sorry!" and she purses her lips. He's about to turn back to his books when the sound comes again, only this time, it's not just a wheezy gasp but some actual words.

"*Leeettttt meeeee oooouuuuuuuutt!*"

The hair stands up on the back of Callum's neck as a cold chill skites up his backbone.

"Who said that?" he says, gazing round in dismay.

"*SHHHHH!*" Miss Duguid is not amused.

"Sorry," says Callum, "but someone—"

"Callum, my dear boy, you *must* be quiet!" scolds the librarian. This makes Mr. Tweed wake up with a snort, and he blinks around, confused.

"Biscuits," he mutters.

Callum is about to break into a smile, when the unearthly voice comes scraching through his mind again.

"*Pleeeasse!*" it hisses. "*I'm ssssssuuuuuffffocating in heeeeeerrrrreee!*" Callum leaps to his feet.

"You MUST have heard that!" he shouts. Mr. Corduroy wakes with a start and falls off his chair.

"What? What? What?" he gasps, struggling up from a rumpled heap. Miss Duguid also stands.

"Callum Maxwell," she says, and the kindly-old-lady-ness is now absent from her voice, "if you carry on like this, I shall have to ask you to *leave!*"

"But—" protests Callum, but he's interrupted.

"*Come onnnnn, Callum.*" The voice is like spiderwebs. "*I neeeeeeedd some SSSSSSUUUUUNNNNN on my leeeeeaaaaavvvvveeeeeessss!*"

"*Leaves?*" shouts Callum.

Both old men struggle to their feet in a cloud of dust and glare at him from under their bushy grey eyebrows. Miss Duguid is now advancing like a sergeant major from behind her desk, and Callum realises it's time to go. As he hastens to the door, he passes the potted cheese plant, and to his open-mouthed astonishment, it says, "*Oh, come ONNNN! Take me wiiiiitttttthhhhh yyooooouuuuuu!*" Shining through every leaf he sees the presence of Things-of-Green and hears a distant cackle as he realises he's been played for an eejit again.

"OUT!" bellows Miss Duguid, propelling him by the collar through the door and out, blinking, into the sunlight. "Come back when you've remembered how to *behave*!" she says primly before retreating back through the door like a hermit crab into its shell.

"That was NOT funny," says Callum crossly to the cackling, shimmering green figure beside him.

"You are mistaken, Callum Maxwell," sings Things-of-Green. "It was very funny indeed!"

Callum has to stifle a grin, despite himself. "Yeah, well, do you make a lot of friends that way?" It's meant as a casual remark, but a cloud passes swiftly over the sun and Things-of-Green stops abruptly in his tracks.

"No," he says, and the music is gone from his voice. "No, not many."

Callum, startled, looks at him and is again struck by the feeling that there is, behind the japery and the trickery, a deep and troubling sadness in this peculiar creature.

"I..." stammers Callum, "I...I didn't *mean* anything by that, it's just..." His voice falters as Things-of-Green continues to stand there like a melancholy sapling on a cold hillside. "Look," says Callum, changing the subject, "why didn't you want me reading those books? I mean, you *were* just deliberately distracting me, weren't you?"

In an instant, the cloud passes as if it had never been there, and Things-of-Green is once again the animated, fluttering mischief-maker of before.

"Ah, *because*, Callum Maxwell, you will learn nothing of value from those books! Written by fools, you see!" There's no anger in the word 'fools', but Callum is surprised.

"You mean, they're wrong about you? About what you are?"

"We never tell fools what we are!"

"So you're not a faery, then?"

Things-of-Green lifts gently on the breeze. "No such thing!" he chirrups. "We are Things-of-Green!"

"Yes," says Callum, exasperated, "but what *are* you?"

Things-of-Green spins lazily in the warm summer air, then faster, then faster, until Callum feels the wind in his face and suddenly finds himself in the centre of a whirling tornado of leaves, flashing past his eyes like fireworks. He has to shield his face from the force of it as a gigantic, booming voice fills his head.

"*We just ARE, Callum Maxwell! WE JUST ARE!*"

And with that, Things-of-Green is gone, leaving Callum quite spectacularly none the wiser.

History 1

Now, some highly unusual things have occurred in this tale so far, but a keen-eyed reader such as yourself will have noticed the oddest, least believable detail of all: namely, that in the time we've known Callum and his friends, it hasn't rained once. Wall-to-wall sunshine, it's been, and this is the west coast of Scotland. Well, it does happen from time to time, and when it does (as you'll have realised) there's nowhere quite as beautiful in all the world.

However, as Callum strolls towards Papa's house from the library, a little put out by Things-of-Green's thrawn contermaciousness but finding it hard to bear a grudge when the whole great grandeur of his wide-eyed surroundings is still embracing him warmly, the sky begins to darken and a low rumble of thunder forewarns a change in the weather. He looks up to see the blue suddenly interrupted by slate-grey clouds the size of battleships, shouldering their way between him and the sun and quite clearly rolling up their sleeves for some seriously overdue rainfall.

As has been the way just lately, Callum feels their attention directly on him, their interest signalled by the rise of a sudden wind, and he is exhilarated and scared in equal measures. The dry summer air is suddenly all a-crackle and he's aware of enormous battling tides in the atmosphere, surging fronts of pressure and temperature squaring up for a major rumble.

Callum's eyes grow wide as he stands, hair tossed by the rising wind, gazing up as the clouds lay down their roiling bulk, enveloping the mountain and blackening the sky still further. All of Skerrils now shivers in the spreading shade, and Callum's spine prickles as he remembers that not all of nature is friendly or indeed safe.

With that thought comes the first raindrop, fat and swollen, splashing against his upturned face and shaking him into action. He shoogles himself from the dwam that's caught him and sprints down the road for Papa's house as the sky thickens with a torrential downpour, wind-driven and blattering and soaking Callum instantly to the bone.

The pavements, still warm from a week of sunshine, stubbornly battle the deluge and send clouds of vapour back into the atmosphere, but it's no use. Within seconds, Callum is charging through an inch of swirling water that bursts upward with every footfall and renders his shoes and socks a spongy, squelching mess.

Callum hoots with ecstatic laughter, holds his arms up against the rain as he runs, and finally makes it, drookit and delighted, to Papa's front door. Hauling it open, he staggers in, water streaming from his hair and his panted greeting swallowed by the hammering of the rain on the roof and windows.

Five minutes later, he is sitting by the streaming window, a towel round his neck and a mug of sweet steaming tea in his hand, Papa chuckling at him through wreaths of pipe smoke.

After Callum has caught his breath and explained his recent cheerfully frustrating conversation with Things-of-Green, he has a question for Papa. It is a very big and important question, and it's not an easy one by any means.

"So I know they're amazing and everything, and they've definitely changed the way the world looks and all that...but are they actually *good*?"

Papa frowns thoughtfully. "Now, why would you be asking *that*, laddie?"

"Well," says Callum slowly, "everything has been amazing since I met them, for sure. And I kind of *think* they're good, you know. But, well, something that can make dogs get up and walk, and make the monument move, and, well, *blow up the school*, for goodness' sake...I get the feeling sometimes that they're really quite dangerous. Especially when they won't tell us what they want, or even what they *are*!"

Papa nods his head slowly and takes a long, thoughtful sook on his pipe. Outside, the rain is still hammering against the windows and it's as dark as dusk though it's not even teatime. Callum sups his tea and waits, till Papa clears his throat.

"Maybe I'll tell you a wee story, Callum," he says. "It'll not answer all your questions but I think that you'll enjoy it. Tell me, what do you know of the Second World War?"

It would be fair to say this was not what Callum was expecting. "Ehm..." he replies, confused, "we did a project on it in Primary six. That was the one with Hitler, wasn't it?"

"Indeed it was, laddie, and a rotten piece of work he was too! Now, when the war began, I was a lad of your age, and I have to say that I didn't think it had a lot to do with me. We weren't a likely target for Nazi bombs, after all, and I was too young to be asked to fight. So I spent my time as I had before, wandering around out on the hills and in the woods and finding caves on the coast, you know. Just like you and your friends today."

Callum grins. "Had you met Things-of-Green by then?" he asks.

Papa's eyes take on a faraway look. "Aye, Callum, I had. Myself and three friends of mine. But that's a tale for another time, so just haud your wheesht a moment!"

Callum apologises and Papa continues.

"Now, you may or may not know that during the war, the Big House at Kinlochree was taken over by the army so that they could train soldiers in the art of wilderness warfare. No, no, laddie, no questions! Drink your tea and listen! I would lie in the heather above the house and watch them doing their exercises. Pretty brutal stuff it was too. They had to jog for miles carrying heavy logs in the pouring rain, that sort of thing. Hand-to-hand combat too, you know, knocking seven bells out of each other. I suppose it doesn't sound very nice to talk about it now, but it was all very exciting at the time. And I picked up a few tips about camouflage too, to be honest, and other things as well.

"They were brave men, anyway, whatever you think about violence and warfare. Some of their names are up on the monument."

Callum nods, enthralled.

"Anyway. Word must have reached the Germans. Don't ask me how. But one moonlit night, I was out camping on the shore near the King's Cave when I was woken by the sound of a boat coming ashore. I rolled into the shade of the big sea-stack down there so I couldn't be seen, and I watched. At first I thought it was some of the soldiers on a night exercise, which they sometimes did, but I could hear them talking and it definitely wasn't our lads. They were speaking in German!"

"*Spies*!" gasps Callum, his eyes wide.

Papa shakes his head. "Worse than that, Callum. Of course, I thought the same as you, but as I watched them, they unloaded an awful lot of equipment from their boat. There were coils of wire, spades and shovels, and big wooden crates of something or other. No, they weren't *spies*, laddie—they were *saboteurs*!"

"What did you do?" asks Callum, his voice barely more than a whisper.

"Well, I had to warn the soldiers, didn't I? I crawled away off the shore as quietly as I could, and when I knew I was out of sight, I got to my feet and ran. I was pelting along up the heather slope, trying to stay low as I ran, feart that the moonlight would show me to the enemy. I was making pretty good progress too, when I turned my ankle in a rabbit hole and clattered to the ground! Completely winded, I was, and my ankle throbbing like a puddock in a pool. I tried to get back up but it was no use, and by this time I could see the Germans moving up the hill.

"Well, now, I couldn't run, I couldn't shout for fear that they'd hear me and finish me off. It was terrible, I was biting my fist in sheer frustration!

"From where I lay, I could see the house, up the hill a ways, and the Germans slinking round it. There were five of them, one carrying a shovel and a roll of wire and two pairs of them lugging these great wooden crates. I was close to tears, Callum, I can tell you!" Papa pauses, gazing through the streaming window and shaking his head. Callum is impatient.

"*Well*?" he prompts.

Papa heaves a deep breath. "Well, indeed. Well, Callum. It was at this point that I was lifted back up to my feet by the heather itself. Swathes of it, sweeping quietly over the hill and wrapping round my shoulders and arms, and lifting me gently to my feet!"

"*Things-of-Green*!" shouts Callum, triumphantly.

"Yes, Callum, Things-of-Green. Not alone, either. There were three of them, I think, swirling around and dancing and popping in and out of sight. Now, I'd only just met them and I was still very impressed with all of this, but I hadn't any time for it at that moment. I pointed to the Germans, who by that time were within about two hundred yards of the house. 'Can you help?' I asked.

"They looked at each other, then they looked at the sky, then they leaped so high in the air I lost sight of them. But within seconds, the moon was completely blotted out by a churning, swirling, shrieking cacophonous flock of birds that came screaming out of nowhere.

"The noise was unbelievable! They clattered out of the sky like a hurricane and just...well, just *slaughtered* the Germans. They seemed to devour them. The sky was black, my eyes, ears, nose and mouth were full of shrieks and feathers. I had to dive to the ground for cover. But in about thirty seconds, it was all quiet again, and when I looked up, the Germans were gone. Nothing left, not even their boots!"

Callum's heart is in his mouth at this astonishing story. "So," he gasps, "they *are* good? I mean, they helped you, didn't they? They saved the soldiers?"

Papa shrugs. "I'm not so sure it's that simple, laddie. I mean, that is what they said they'd done when they reappeared, and they were obviously very pleased with themselves. I must admit I was amazed and delighted, and I did think they had saved the day. But it was pretty brutal. It was...well, it wasn't *human*, if you know what I mean."

Papa pauses again, and Callum senses a darkness in the room, beyond that cast by the storm still raging outside.

"Anyway, I thanked them from the bottom of my heart and limped home feeling deeply blessed for knowing these incredible beings. But the next day, word came round Skerrils that three soldiers had gone missing from the house at Kinlochree. They had gone out on a scouting mission and never come back. One witness claimed they'd been carried away by an enormous flock of birds, but he was dismissed as a lunatic!

"It turned out, not that I could *tell* anyone, of course, that Things-of-Green had enjoyed getting rid of the Germans so much he'd decided to do it again to someone else! It didn't make any difference to him that the first people had been enemies and the others were friends. I tried to explain it to him and he just laughed!"

A shudder runs through Callum as he thinks of his *own* friends, whom he hasn't seen for a few hours now. "What happened?" he whispers. "Did...did they bring the soldiers back?"

Papa shakes his head. "Never seen again. *Their* names are up there on the monument with the rest of them!"

As the full weight of this story settles on Callum's shoulders, the storm outside stops abruptly and a piercing shaft of sunlight slants in the window.

"Thanks for the tea, Papa," he says, getting to his feet with a sense of purpose. "I think I'd better go and find my friends."

Music

Somewhat shaken, Callum makes his way up the high street as the clock tower chimes five o'clock. Vicky should be finished at the old folks' home, so he heads in that direction to catch her as she walks home. The sun has come out again with full force, and the only hint of the recent downpour is the merry trickle of water down rone pipes and a rising muggy dampness in the air. Birds are singing enthusiastically and the whole world looks as if it's had a fresh lick of paint.

It's not long before the clouds have lifted from Callum's thoughts just as surely as they have from the mountaintop, and he is once again dazzled and delighted by the great cheerful chiming of the world around him. Warm summer smells fill his nostrils and his skin tingles with excitement.

With a spring in his step, he rounds the corner and steps onto the well-cut lawn that surrounds the old folks' home, bounces up to the front door and steps in to reception. A tired-looking woman in a blue uniform is sitting behind the desk, and she looks at Callum enquiringly.

"Hiya," says Callum. "I'm just wondering if Vicky's finished with her music yet?"

The woman behind the desk looks surprised. "Oh, yes. She only came for about twenty minutes today. She was playing away as usual, on the fiddle this time, and then about halfway through a song, she just stopped, smiled and walked out! Look, she even left her fiddle!" She points at a chair in the corner, and sure enough, there sits Vicky's violin.

All the apprehension is suddenly back in Callum's mind and he almost shouts, "Which way did she go?"

A little taken aback, the woman gestures vaguely in the direction of the path which snakes away from town and leads through heather and gullies right up onto the mountain ridge.

With a muttered "Thanks," Callum bursts back out the door and sprints off up the path, not at all sure what he's afraid of but filled with a weird foreboding all the same. As he runs, scattering small birds in his wake and pushing through the tangles of meadowsweet and waving grasses which press on the path from both sides, he angrily wonders what exactly the *point* of all of this is. What good is it doing him, knowing Things-of-Green and all his wretched cronies? What actual good is it doing any of them?

On he runs, his heart pounding and his breath coming in frantic gasps as the path rises steeply and the town dwindles away below him. Callum knows this path well, or at least this stretch of it. The whole path goes on for miles and miles and miles, but this first section leads up to the Corrie of the Dubh Loch, and Callum and Steven have camped by the silvery lochan more than once. Callum's not at all sure why Vicky would be heading this way, but he is in no doubt at all that this is where she is going. He charges on as if carried by some unknown force, determined to find his friend and make absolutely sure no harm comes to her.

Finally, after running hard for nearly twenty minutes over landscape that has risen from grass to heather to rocks, and with sweat streaming down him, Callum crests a small rise and comes into sight of the Dubh Loch. The great grey corrie rises over it, encircling the glittering waters like the wall of some dark, looming fortress, the unbroken blue vastness of the sky above interrupted only by a circling raven whose low croak reaches Callum through the humid air.

Stopping for a moment to catch his breath and to wipe the sweat from his eyes, Callum scans his surroundings for some sign of Vicky. Far below him in the direction from which he has run, he can see the monument, and beyond that the town, almost invisible in the heat haze. The sea is a jewelled mirror sparkling off to a shimmering horizon, the dark bulk of MacArthur's Island hunkered in the bay like a sleeping dragon.

For a brief moment, Callum feels dizzy, as if he could just fall off the hillside and tumble into the giant sky's waiting embrace, but he is called back to himself by a shout from above.

"Callum! Callum! Over here!"

Spinning round, Callum sees movement about halfway up the jagged rock face on the north side of the corrie. With a surge of relief, he realises it is Vicky, waving down at him and evidently quite all right.

It takes Callum a further ten minutes to reach her, picking round the lochan's rocky shore then scrambling up the rough, uneven stone of the cliff. He finds he is following the course of a trickling burn that flows from some unknown spring higher up the mountain, sometimes disappearing completely under the rocks only to reappear further up.

At last, exhausted and scart-handed, he arrives at Vicky's side. She's sitting on a broad, flat boulder, which is warm from the sun and commands a stunning view down into the corrie and beyond. Callum collapses breathlessly on his back, the warmth of the stone soothing his aching muscles and the heavy stillness of the air settling on him like a comfort blanket.

"Ready?" asks Vicky.

Callum sits up abruptly. "What?" he gasps.

Vicky looks impatient. "Are you *ready*?" she repeats. "You'd better be ready. It's going to happen in about two minutes flat."

This is rather confusing, even by Vicky's high standards, but Callum can't be bothered to argue; he's just relieved she's okay. Well, as okay as she ever is.

Vicky rattles on. "Isn't it *incredible*? I mean, I thought I knew music before we met these things, but...well, *WOW*!"

Ah, thinks Callum, *so this* is *about Things-of-Green and the others*. A little note of worry awakens at the back of his mind: *what have they told Vicky?*

Before he can express his concerns, however, Vicky has handed him a stout wooden pole about the same height as himself and is bustling him over to another boulder which sits at the top of a steep stone chute. All the while she is blethering away under her breath, saying things like, "A wee bit more to the left," and, "Unbelievable! This is going to be *unbelievable*!"

At last, she has Callum where she wants him and has indicated that at her signal he is to lever the big boulder out of its resting place and send it tumbling down the scree towards the lochan.

"Why can't *you* do it?" asks Callum, a bit rattled and also sort of thinking that Vicky might at least have said 'hello'. "I mean, whatever it is—"

"*Look*," snaps Vicky, "I've been up here for three hours getting this sorted out. Every single detail. And it's been bloody hard work! They've shown me which rocks to move, which burn to dam, which crevasses to stuff with heather, but I've had to sort it all myself! Now, I'm not complaining because this is going to be amazing, but if I ask for a bit of help, one *tiny wee bit of help*, do you think you could maybe just do it without jabbering at me?"

"Sorry," says Callum, half laughing. "I'll shunt the boulder. What are you doing?"

"Unblocking the dam!" chirrups Vicky, perfectly happy again and bounding off some distance to where she has blocked the burn to form a tranquil, silver pool in a rocky hollow. "Oh, look, *look*!"

She points down the hillside, and Callum sees the heather bouncing in a sudden warm, rolling wind, moving in waves up the mountain towards them.

"Ten seconds!" yelps Vicky. "Nine, eight, seven..." The rising wind has reached the lochan and is tickling the waters into motion, ripples spreading in wide arcs and sparkling wavelets breaking on the shore below them. "Three, two, one...*NOW*!"

Callum heaves his boulder, Vicky breaks the dam, the wind balloons up around them and the raven's croak echoes back and forth across the corrie, and suddenly, suddenly, the whole mountainside is reverberating with a deafening, sonorous music of a beauty Callum can barely comprehend. The tumbling boulder has dislodged a cascade of scree which booms and crashes in a thundering descent, a timpanous, tempestuous percussion which awakens every echo in the circling cliff.

Meanwhile, the rush of water from the unblocked dam creates first a musical swoosh and then, as it forces the air through the rocks and crags, a great trumpeting blast of notes like a gargantuan heavenly fanfare. The wind itself, split and swirled by the jagged rocks, becomes a many-voiced choir, frantic, lamenting, ecstatic and wild.

There are other sounds, other voices, lifting and echoing from cliff to corrie to lochan to sky, and the raven, joined now by its mate, circles effortlessly in the vibrating air and croaks its hoarse harmonies in delight. The music can be felt in every bone; it courses through the blood and fills the heart fit to burst it.

For a moment, Callum, giddy and reeling, almost hears words in the swelling song, phrases he can half understand. He looks at Vicky's rapturous expression, at the tears streaming freely from her closed eyes, and he realises that the music is perfect as it is and needs no more meaning than the sheer sweet sound of it.

For two full minutes, the mountainous symphony rises and grows, and both Callum and Vicky have to sit down for sheer awe. Then, in one last crag-blown crescendo, it ends, leaving only echoes, an occasional crass rattle of scree and the memory of something impossibly beautiful.

Callum realises he hasn't breathed since the music began, and he heaves a huge, cool sigh. Vicky does the same and wipes the tears from her face without embarrassment.

"Well," she says in a shaky voice, "I do believe that is the first time I have played a mountain!"

Creid

For several long minutes, they lie on the warm, rough surface of the boulder, allowing the silence to settle on them as the last sweet reverberations of the music disappear, when they are suddenly aware of movement on the ridge above them. Callum reluctantly sits up and looks round, raising his arm to shield his eyes from the sun. Edging slowly down the rocky slope towards them is a figure, silhouetted against the bright, blue sky. Callum gets to his feet and Vicky sits up.

"Is that..." she begins.

"It's Craig!" Callum cries. The pair of them bellow a cheery greeting to their friend, but it soon becomes clear that all is not well. Craig is staggering down the scree in a dwam, looking lost and dazed. He stumbles amongst the jagged rocks and almost falls, but Callum leaps to his side and offers a steadying hand.

"What's up?" Callum asks, alarmed.

Craig looks at him blankly; he is deathly pale. Vicky's up too by now, putting an arm round Craig's shoulder and ushering him to the rock to sit down.

"The...the *blood*!" mutters Craig. Vicky and Callum exchange a startled glance.

"What blood?" asks Callum. "What are you talking about, Craig? Where have you *been*?"

"Hundreds of them!" Craig goes on as if he doesn't even know his friends are there. "*Hundreds* of them! And they just... They just *killed* them! Killed *all* of them!" Although it doesn't seem possible, he turns even paler, and his brown eyes roll back in his head as if he's about to faint.

"He's going," says Vicky in a low voice, before giving him a shake. "*Craig*!" she shouts. "*Craig*!"

Craig's eyes briefly come back into focus. "Cr...Cr..." he stammers.

"What's he doing?" asks Callum in alarm. "Is he trying to remember his name? How could he forget his own name?"

"Cr...Cr..." whispers the poor stricken figure, sinking slowly backwards, his eyes rolling again. "*Cr...Creid*!" With that, Craig flops onto the boulder like a sack of tatties, unconscious.

Moments later, Callum is scrabbling up the scree in the direction Craig came from, his heart pounding in fear at what he might find and his mind buzzing in confusion at what *creid* might mean. He can hear Vicky singing quietly to Craig below, a kind of reverse lullaby, trying to urge him to wake up. All the blessed peace and magic of the musical mountain seems to have vanished, and Callum feels danger and threat all around him.

The fear lends him speed, and he is able to crest the ridge in a matter of minutes. Bracing for the sight of some horrifying massacre, he takes a deep breath and looks down into the glen on the other side of the ridge.

For one giddying moment, he has the horrible impression of a scene awash with blood, crow-pecked bodies scattered and piled by broken swords and the rising wail of abandoned women and children. Callum's blood freezes, but even as he feels his stomach heaving in revulsion, the scene begins to wobble, fade, and then melt into the landscape like butter into toast.

All that remains is a gentler slope than the one he has climbed, a grassy hillside split by glistening burns with the occasional rowan tree shaking its leaves in the light breeze. Far below, the hillside spreads out into a broad moorland, a patchwork of bracken and heather, the odd wee sparkling pool ringed by alders and silver birch. Here and there are the ruins of old buildings, little more than rectangles of coarse boulders, sunk so far into the land that it is now impossible to guess what the buildings once were.

There is absolutely no sign of any trouble at all. In fact, the scene is one of wide tranquillity, and Callum's head spins in astonishment. He flops to his knees, panting for breath, his muscles burning.

"Did they like it?"

Callum near jumps out of his skin in shock. The voice has come from just over his shoulder, a smooth, rolling, grinding sound like curling stones sliding over ice. Callum spins around but there's no-one there, just the rocky ridge.

"Who—"

He stops as a man-sized boulder detaches itself from the crags, turns to him, and repeats, "Did they like it?"

Even after everything, the sight and sound of Things-of-Stone chills Callum to the bone. There is something about him that is just plain scary. Where Things-of-Green and Things-of-Blood burble with a deep and mischievous humour—not entirely *safe,* certainly, but kind of understandable if you put your reason on hold for a bit—Things-of-Stone seems cold, alien. *Fell,* to use the old word.

Callum watches, agog, as the big stone figure crumbles to pebbles and flows towards him, stopping and reforming into a dark monolith before him.

"D...d...did *who* like *what*?" he gasps.

"Craig." The word reaches Callum's ears like windblown sand. "Did they like seeing the battle?"

And of course, things become a bit clearer. These baffling, infuriating creatures have decided to put on a wee show for Craig, and in the process have near enough fried the poor lad's brain. Anger rises in Callum's chest.

"What have you done to him?" he demands. Then, as an afterthought, he adds, "And why do you keep saying 'did *they* like it'? Craig's just one person!"

Things-of-Stone tilts his head, looking, for a moment, like an inquisitive bird, or at least like a terrifying giant statue of an inquisitive bird.

"We do not understand," he grinds.

"Oh, never mind," snaps Callum. "Just tell me what you did with him!"

Startlingly, the rocky face that Callum has been talking to is...just a rocky face, uninhabited by any intelligence—nothing more than a jagged outcrop on a jagged ridge. Things-of-Stone's voice now comes from a point behind him, and Callum spins round to see another animated boulder, about five yards away, gazing down to the moorland below.

"How did you..." gasps Callum, then gives up. He realises he may as well just wait for an answer; these creatures do not seem to respond to anything as normal as a straight question.

"We believe that the ones you call Craig are warriors. They like war. Is this not so?"

Callum can't think what on earth the creature is talking about, until a memory of Craig sitting at the monument and merrily blasting his way through countless alien and zombie armies on his phone comes to mind.

"He likes *games*, if that's what you mean!"

"We showed them games," comes the reply. "Games *we* used to play. Like the ones called Craig, we used to do battle. We used the kilted ones, and the painted ones, and the ones with metal plates. We used the fisherfolk, the herdsfolk. Great games we played. We showed Craig. We thought they would enjoy it."

Callum's not sure if it's his imagination or if a note of sulky glumphiness has entered the weird, scraping voice.

"They were supposed to enjoy it," he says again.

"But for goodness' sake," shouts Callum, "*why*? I mean, what's the point? What did you want from him?"

Things-of-Stone turns his huge, dark head towards Callum.

"*Creid*," he rumbles. Then the boulder is once again a boulder, and Callum knows he is alone on the ridge.

Selkies

Callum sleeps in the following morning, bone-weary from the exertions of the day before. Although Craig had eventually woken up, Callum and Vicky had more or less had to humph him down the hill between them and, as Vicky was kind enough to point out, he weighed a blinking ton. Not only that but he was gibbering the whole way about the horrific bloodshed he had witnessed, and saying "*Creid, creid, creid*" over and over again which, since neither Vicky nor Callum knew what it meant, wasn't terribly helpful.

So here's Callum, quilt over his head and snoring though it's past nine o' clock. That and the sound of a light drizzle rattling on the skylight create a peaceful drone which is rudely shattered when his bedroom door bursts open and Steven barges in.

"Callum!" he bellows. "Wake up! We've got to go!"

Callum, who was having a lovely dream in which he kept finding huge pots full of money, leaps in fright and cracks his head against the sloping ceiling of his attic room.

"OW!" he yells, grasping his head with both hands and promptly falling out of bed with a thump. His duvet flops on top of him, and for an entertaining second or two he is entangled like a fish in a net, kicking and struggling in wounded startlement.

"Stop messing around and hurry up," says Steven unsympathetically. "I'll be waiting downstairs!"

Callum finally extricates himself from his bedclothes, sits up, rubs his eyes and gives a deep sigh. Friends can be hard work sometimes, he thinks.

Shortly afterwards, he's dressed and sitting at the breakfast table, with Steven pacing impatiently behind him. He's just about managed to shake the sleep out of his bones and is beginning to take an interest in the land of the living.

"What's the big hurry, anyway?" he asks through a mouthful of toast.

"Things-of-Water!" says Steven.

It's enough to make Callum gulp down the last of his breakfast and leap to his feet, knocking his chair over in his haste. Another adventure, another day in this mysteriously blessed world, another step toward understanding the bizarre, interfering brilliance of these creatures.

"Why didn't you say so?" he shouts, grabbing Steven by the shoulder and pulling him out the back door. The two of them run, hooting with laughter, down the

High Street, arms raised and fingers spread to feel the delicious drizzling rain that gusts around them.

The rest of the good people of Skerrils are less enthusiastic, and the boys speed past huddled figures with upturned collars, shoulders hunched against the weather. Mr. MacQuarrie, the miserable minister, stalks past under a black umbrella, offering the boys a scowl as they skid round the corner into Gilmartin Street and on towards the shore. They hear the waves surging against the shingle, and the sound draws them onward like the merry tinkling music of the ice cream van. However, as they pass Papa's cottage, a thought occurs to Callum and he stumbles to a halt, trainers skiting on the wet pavement.

"Hold on!" he shouts to Steven, who stops and turns impatiently.

"What?"

"I've just got to ask Papa something," replies Callum breathlessly, and he steps up to the door and walks in.

"*Papa!*" he calls, and is answered by a warm "Hello!" from the front room. Callum steps in, politely declining Papa's offer of a seat and a cup of tea. "Sorry, Papa, I've no time today. I just need to ask you something!"

The old man leans forward with interest. "Go ahead, laddie."

Callum takes a deep breath.

"What," he asks, "does '*creid*' mean?"

Well, before Papa answers he wants the lowdown on exactly *why* Callum would ask that, so as hastily as he can, Callum recounts the events of the day before. Papa listens with keen attention, and to Callum's dismay, he seems to grow pale as he hears of Craig's terrifying experience.

"Ach," he mutters under his breath. "Will they never learn?" He puts his teacup down and grips the arms of his chair so tightly his knuckles go white.

"Learn what? What does it mean, Papa? Is it Gaelic?" Callum's questions come rapidly, impatiently. He can see Steven through the window, pacing back and forth in the rain, and he urgently wants to be off. Something in Papa's look, though, tells him this is important.

"Aye, Callum, it's Gaelic. It means 'believe'."

"*Believe?*" gasps Callum. "What sort of message is that?" To his growing dismay, Papa's face suddenly becomes worn and haggard, and he slumps back in his chair with a defeated sigh.

"Callum," he begins, but he's interrupted by Steven banging on the window and shouting in, his voice muffled through the glass.

"*Hurry UP, Callum!*" he shouts. "*We're keeping him waiting!*" The manic light in Steven's eyes is in such contrast with the slumped figure of Papa in the chair that Callum is briefly paralysed in confusion.

"Papa," he says, but stops as the old man raises a hand.

"It's okay, son," says Papa in a low voice. "Go. But, Callum?"

"Yes?"

"*Come back.* Whatever it is you're about to see, you come back here afterwards to tell me about it. Do you understand?"

Callum is agitated. He's never heard Papa talking like this before. "Of course," he says, but there's doubt in his voice. Papa thumps the arm of his chair with his fist, sending a plume of dust swirling into the light cast through the window.

"*Promise!*" he shouts. Callum jumps. "*Promise* me, Callum. You *must* come back. I'll explain everything to you, but you *must come back*!"

Callum, shaken, promises and means it.

Finally, he's back out with Steven, and if the strange encounter with Papa had rather taken the wind out of his sails, a couple of seconds in Steven's company swiftly puffs them back up again. Callum pushes his lingering concern for Craig to the back of his mind and allows himself to be caught up in Steven's wilful exuberance.

"Here we GOOO!" yells Steven, and they sprint off together, gathering enough speed to leap right over the sea wall without stopping. They land four-square in the glistening shingle with the salt tang of the whipping waves in their nostrils. Off they charge, round the coastline, Callum not even bothering to ask where they're going as the drizzling smir mingles with the sea spray to turn their world to a sparkling blur. It's the first truly choppy day in weeks, and the sea is grey and white, churning and crashing in the wind as if applauding the boys' exhilarating flight.

On they pound, jumping from the shingle up to the rock pool crags, leaping like mountain goats over the barnacled rocks as the town disappears behind them, now using hands and feet to scrabble up and over the great layered promontories which pile and fold along the shore towards the base of the cliffs. At sea level, these jutting fingers of stone are covered in seaweed, limpets, mussels and sea anemones, but the boys climb up over the tide line to where the rock is rough with lichen, painting the surface in yellows and purples.

They scrabble over one of these natural walls, then another, each one taking them further from any sign of civilisation. The narrow channels between are surging with the foamy sea, and now and again a wave slaps the stone with such vigour that a big curtain of spray shoots up around the laughing boys.

At last, Steven stops by the side of a wide, dark rock pool, and Callum breathlessly catches up and stands beside him. They are almost at the cliffs, close enough to hear the mewling seabirds, the kittiwakes and guillemots, and to smell the acrid whiff of their wind-spattered droppings. Both boys are grinning expectantly, certain they're about to be treated to a fresh round of uncanny magic. They don't have long to wait.

As Callum scans the surroundings, squinting against the wind, his gaze is drawn by something in the rock pool. It is Steven's reflection, split and scattered in the rippling water, but that's not what is odd about it. No, it seems to be growing, stretching down, deep into the black water.

"Ehm, Steven," says Callum, but his friend has clearly noticed too and has taken a step back in surprise. The reflection, however, does not follow suit. Instead, it continues to grow, to spread and darken.

"This is interesting," says Steven with a manic grin, just as the reflection decides to abandon all pretence and rise up out of the rock pool in front of them. There it stands, shimmering, silver and smiling.

"Things-of-Water!" cry both boys together, and the figure bows its head.

"Are you ready?" it says, its voice like a rushing river. It raises one swirling, misty arm and gestures to the waves beyond, which seem to rise and fall at its command.

Callum's gaze follows the gesture and he sees an object in the waves, black and sleek and round. At first, he thinks it's a buoy like the ones the fishermen tie to their lobster creels. But then he sees another, and another, and another, and now he can make out the deep, dark eyes, the whiskers, and he feels himself observed by a host of intelligent creatures.

"Seals!" he shouts in delight. "Steven, look!"

By now, there are hundreds of them visible, rising and falling in mesmerising harmony with the cold grey water, all watching them, all waiting.

Steven is enraptured. "Not seals," he replies, like someone in a trance. "Selkies!" And he raises his arms high above his head, steps to the edge of the rock and dives, vanishing in a circle of foam beneath the icy waves.

Doubt

"*teven!*" yells Callum in horror, scrambling down as close to the surging water as he dares. "STEEEVEENN!!" He daren't even blink as he searches the restless surface of the waves, waiting for his friend to reappear, but with no luck. His stinging eyes are met only with the deep stares of the selkies, who still seem to be waiting. "STEEEE—" His third cry is interrupted by a wave which slaps him heartily across the chops. Coughing and spluttering, Callum claws his way back up the rock to wipe his eyes.

"Why do you not follow?"

Callum staggers to his feet, and there stands Things-of-Water, shining and refracting the spiralling drizzle and the heaving sea.

"He'll drown!" gasps Callum, struggling to look at the strange being without feeling giddy. Things-of-Water rises and falls in front of him like a roiling wave in what Callum realises is laughter. The voice tinkles like icicles tumbling in a spring thaw.

"*Believe*, Callum Maxwell," it says, and the voice is so full of merriment and life that Callum finds himself grinning excitedly.

"Och, what the heck, I'm soaked anyway!" he cries, and with that, he holds his nose and *leaps* out into the sea after his friend.

The shock of the freezing water as it closes over his head punches all the breath out of Callum's body in a pluming silver mushroom of bubbles, and his first instinct is to struggle for the surface to gulp down some air. As he is about to do so, however, strong hands grasp his arms. It's only then he realises his eyes are closed. He opens them in surprise and stares in awe at the sight that meets him.

Rather than the grey-blue blur he expects to see underwater, his vision is crystal clear, and the water glints and fractures around him in a symphony of silver. Right in front of him, holding his arms, is Steven, grinning silently from ear to ear, his clothes slowly rippled by invisible currents. Behind Steven, a host of selkies swirl and glide through the icy water. They swoop towards the boys at speed, only turning aside with an effortless twist of a flipper when they are close enough for Callum to be buffeted in their wake.

Deep, deep below them, Callum can see a sandy seafloor, criss-crossed by rocky reefs alive with starfish and sea urchins. Every surface dances with dividing diamonds of light that streak down from the restless surface above them. Without even realising he is doing it, Callum draws a deep, sucking breath, and the whole sea seems to surge through him, replacing his blood with icy brine, clearing his mind, clearing his vision, claiming him as its own.

"Isn't it amazing?" Steven's voice sounds inside Callum's head, although his lips don't move. *Ah, so we're psychic as well now, are we?* thinks Callum, so far beyond surprise that it barely even registers when Steven replies, "Looks like it!"

Selkies appear at either side of the boys, and they realise they are being invited to follow. The boys extend their arms out in front of them in proper superhero mode and weave and fly through the water with the same ease as their solemn new companions.

The feeling of freedom is utterly overwhelming, and for a while all the boys can do is loop-the-loop and dive and swoop in sheer, giddying *joy*, until at last they notice the host of selkies waiting patiently for them to come along. Callum and Steven look at each other, their faces still split with grins, nod and follow.

They become part of a great school of seal-folk, pushing forwards through the bright sea, scattering shoals of fish like fractured metallic rainbows. Kelp forests wave in the tide beneath them, dotted with the unblinking eyes of eels and crabs, and purple jellyfish gently balloon in their wake.

Something looms out of the blue before them, and at first it looks like one of the rocky crags, jewelled with mussels and barnacles, but as they draw closer, there's something about the shape that doesn't fit. It is weirdly familiar, and it doesn't look as if it is made from rock; it's more like wood.

"Is it a shipwreck?" thinks Callum. He turns an enquiring look on Steven, who has stopped dead, hovering dumbly with a look of doitit bemusement on his face.

"No," comes his voice in Callum's head. "It's not *a* shipwreck. It's..."

The penny drops, and Callum doesn't need any more explanation. Rising from the white sand of the seafloor is a huge, wooden *throne* constructed from the remains of every boat Steven has ever tried to sail to MacArthur's Island. The shimmering crowd of selkies has parted to create a clear path, and the boys can't help but come to the conclusion that they want Steven to go and *sit* on the throne.

"Do they..." thinks Callum in amused confusion, "do they think you were giving them those boats as a gift?"

Whatever the facts of the matter, it can't be denied that the solemn seal-faces are looking at Steven expectantly and that, under the circumstances, it would be terribly rude of him not to go and have a seat. Always a considerate young man, Steven gives the best shrug he can manage underwater and glides smoothly over to the throne.

Callum watches, half laughing, half bewildered, as his friend settles himself on the strange structure with perfect ease, as if being enthroned under the waves were the most natural thing in the world. A ripple moves through the gathered crowd of seal-folk, and Callum follows it to see a huge shape emerging from the deep-blue gloom behind the throne.

Swimming towards them, slowly, sedately, is a seal four or five times the size of any of the others. Its whiskers are grey and impossibly bushy, and Callum is struck by the sense that it is enormously old, but that is not the strangest thing about it. The strangest thing about it is that, between its front flippers, it is carrying a sparkling, spiralling seashell crown which catches every slanting shaft of light. This vast, ancient creature of the deep slowly swims towards Steven, and Callum is propelled forward and down as four selkies behind him urge him to kneel before the throne.

"*Welcome*," comes a voice in Callum's head, echoing as if through the timeless caverns of the deep. "*Welcome home!*"

To Callum's consternation, Steven raises a regal hand with a look on his face that says "This is all quite right and proper!"

The great grey seal flows forward and deftly drops the crown on Steven's head. Other, smaller seals have now swum up behind Callum and are draping him with long fronds of seaweed till he looks like some bizarre marine courtier to the Great King Steven.

Callum looks around at the impossible myriad of ocean creatures circling the throne: lobsters, scallops, creeping flounders and rippling rays, raising the sand in billowing clouds as they creep closer to the throne. There is a deep, intense sense that some kind of order is being restored, that it is good and correct that Steven (daft, glaikit, boat-sinking *Steven*, for goodness' sake!) should sit in state before them all like the emperor of the ocean.

And suddenly, despite the hypnotic swirling light, despite the slow, stately progress of the gathered creatures around him, despite the deep, wise eyes of their selkie hosts, Callum is unable to shake the notion that this is all completely, wildly *ridiculous*. This is no place for him; he's promised Papa he'll be back, after all. Also, the thought of his daft wee pal suddenly lording it up to a bunch of haddock is too much, and he laughingly tries to think a message to Steven to explain why they should be off.

But then he's not laughing at all, because the last breath he drew was suddenly not the refreshing draft of the last few minutes; it was salty, unwelcoming, deadly cold seawater, and it's pushed its way into lungs which are now desperate, *desperate* for air.

Horrified, Callum looks wildly round at a crowd of unfriendly alien faces, the slow-gathering homage of moments before transformed into a gathering army of angry, hungry creatures. Panicked, he kicks out for the surface and is only now aware of how heavy and clinging his clothes are, and of how far away the surface is.

Blood pounding in his ears, Callum frantically kicks and thrashes his way up, the pressure in his lungs unbearable, the urge to cough up the water almost too much to bear. Below him, Steven retains an eerie calm, as if Callum's fate is no longer his problem, and Callum's mind just has time (between flashing his life before his eyes) to call Steven every treacherous wee toerag under the sun.

Just when it feels as if the need to breathe is too much to bear, Callum breaks the surface and gasps, huge lungfuls of cold, salty air. The weather has not improved during his time underwater, and there is now a ferocious gale whipping up the surface of the sea. Worse than that, Callum cannot find the shore as a deep, dense haar has descended over the water and he can only see a few feet in any direction.

Trusting himself to fate, he launches out in a vigorous front crawl, trying to ignore the dead weight of his sodden clothes and his waterlogged trainers. Every breath is interrupted by a slapping wave, and he coughs and splutters in the cruel salt spray. He feels as if he's swallowed half the Atlantic, and that, coupled with the constant rise and fall of the waves, is threatening to engulf him in a whammlin queasiness that can only have one outcome.

After what seems like an eternity of misery, Callum becomes aware of the sound of waves crashing on rocks. This brings two thoughts: one, that he must be getting close to shore (good); and two, that when he gets there, there is every chance he will be pounded to a pulp on the cruel black rocks (not so good).

He briefly toys with the idea of changing course, attempting to swim round the coast till he comes to the more welcoming shingle, but he's so wretchedly exhausted that he's pretty sure he'll drown before he gets there. Also, to his rage and astonishment, he realises he's actually being deliberately pushed towards the rocks; every other wave bears the grinning, expectant face of Things-of-Water, and Callum understands he is in the hands of a power that does not care for him at all.

Even in this impossible situation, Callum finds he has reserves of strength he had never guessed before, and that they can be tapped through the power of complete and total fury.

"*Leave me alone!*" he bellows. "*I'm NOT YOURS!*" Coughing and gagging on the freezing water, he continues to shout and rage, even as he sees the black jagged cliffs looming ever closer. "*Leave me ALONE!*"

But even the energy of blind wrath has to give way at some point, and poor Callum is spent. He gives another feeble slap to the surface of the water, casts a final, desperate look up into the grey, hazy sky, then sinks beneath into the swallowing silence and is spun and tumbled onto the rocks like a piece of helpless flotsam.

Part 3

The Trog

"Promise me, Callum. You MUST come back!"

Callum has no idea how long he has been unconscious, but he is suddenly aware that he is not unconscious anymore. He sits up, Papa's voice echoing in his head, and looks around in confusion. He has an odd sense of some terrible danger having been avoided, and is completely baffled to find himself dry and reasonably warm. As he blinks and rubs his eyes, he can hear the distant pounding of the waves, but it seems a mercifully long way off.

So where is he? It's dark and still, but for the dancing flames of a merry fire a few paces away from him. He's lying on what seems to be a huge fur blanket thrown over a flat rock, and there are two or three more blankets draped over him. As his eyes adjust to the dim light, he can see the shadows the fire is casting onto high rock walls, and he realises he is deep inside a cave. He also realises that he is not alone; sitting quietly on the other side of the fire is a strange, squat figure.

"Hello?" says Callum, climbing painfully to his feet. The figure doesn't move. Callum notices his clothes are laid out on a rock by the fire and are steaming away pleasantly, which makes him wonder what he has on. He looks down and finds he is dressed, or rather wrapped, in a bizarre mish-mash of rags, fur and feathers, woven together with grass or straw and hung with seashells and shiny pebbles.

Now, if this had been the oddest thing to happen to Callum today, he would probably have thought more of it. Since he has just narrowly escaped being killed by a watery spirit, who was annoyed because Callum was insufficiently impressed by its attempt to ensnare him in an undersea kingdom ruled over by one of his friends in a seashell hat on a throne made of his own rubbish sunken boats, Callum just gives a shrug and carries on.

"Hello?" he says again. "Excuse me?" He doesn't feel any fear as he's decided this strange wee character must have pulled him out of the water and so probably doesn't mean him any harm. Still, he doesn't wish to startle the little chap, so he moves cautiously towards the fire to get a better look at him.

He is crouched on his haunches, his eyes closed and his hands extended towards the fire. The man is very old; he has a long, scraggly, grey beard, and his fingers are as thin and bony as the claws of a bird. The top of his head is as bald as a bowling ball and glints warmly in the firelight, but long, tangled, grey hair extends from the back of his head and hangs round his shoulders in knotted, shaggy locks. He is dressed in an outfit similar to Callum's, although the man's is just about recognisable as trousers and a kind of bodywarmer, rather than the shapeless blanket he's wrapped around his guest.

As Callum takes another step towards him, the figure opens his sparkling eyes and turns his head.

"You're awake!" he cries in a funny, high-pitched voice that makes Callum think the man hasn't had much practice at talking for a while. "You are awake, awake, awake," he continues, rising to his feet and hopping about in delight. "Welcome! All blessings on you, friend, all blessings!"

Callum has to stifle a chuckle at the wee man's cavorting. "Aye. Ehm, thanks very much for saving me!"

The man nods vigorously. He seems to be performing some sort of ritual—tapping the stone floor, then tapping the walls, then reaching up to tap the low ceiling—all the while mumbling something to himself and shoogling the various bits of feather and shell that dangle from his outfit.

"What are you doing, by the way?" asks Callum.

Startlingly, the little figure stops and stares at him, then bounds over with unexpected agility so he can whisper urgently in Callum's ear, "*I am giving THANKS!*"

Callum gets a noseful of the man's breath, which isn't great, and he's about to pull away when his host is off again, finishing his strange ceremony. This takes about three more minutes, during which Callum realises he is in the home of the Trog, the semi-legendary wild man of a dozen playground games. 'Trog Touch'—the game in which whoever is 'it' has to pass the jandie-laden Trog Touch to his fleeing friends by slapping imaginary bugs off their backs—is one of several examples that Callum decides not to share with his new friend.

At last, the Trog straightens up and comes to Callum's side with a hand extended politely. This sudden switch to gentlemanly good manners is a little jarring, but Callum's weird-o-meter is still riding high so he accepts the hand without a second thought. The Trog shakes his hand warmly.

"Welcome," he says again, "and how are you feeling?"

"Fine, thanks," says Callum, and he's a little surprised to discover this is actually true. "I must admit, I thought I was a goner there!"

"No, no, no," chuckles the Trog. "That was just their way of playing with you!"

It takes Callum a moment to figure out that the Trog is talking about Things-of-Water, and he is astonished.

"Wait a second!" he shouts. "Can you see them too?"

The Trog bows his head and clasps his hands together in front of his chest. "See, hear, feel, smell, taste the Great Ones, *yes*!" he cries, and suddenly he's off again, hopping round the cave, picking up stray bits of pebble and shell and piling them neatly on rock ledges around the walls. "Give thanks, give thanks," he sings to himself in his scratchy, wee voice, the fire casting his giant shadow up the craggy walls.

After what feels like about an hour and a half, Callum begins to feel a bit impatient.

"Look," he says, "ehm, thanks for saving me and everything, but I think I'd better be getting home now."

This seems to snap the Trog back out of his reverie, and he straightens up again and returns to Callum's side.

"Oh, of course, of course!" He giggles. "My apologies! I can give thanks later, when you're gone. Follow me!" With that, he skips off down a dark, damp passageway, leaving Callum barely enough time to slip back into his dry clothes and follow the Trog into the darkness.

It's pitch-black in the tunnel, and Callum has to grope his way forwards. Helpfully, though, the Trog spends the whole journey singing an odd little song, and the sound of it gives Callum something to aim for. The song echoes back off the slimy walls, and to

Callum's confused ears it sounds as if the Trog is singing:

Hold by end indicated,
Remove lid or cap,
Use striker to ignite
Hold away from body!

He is chanting the words with deep solemnity, over and over again.

If Callum wasn't sure before, he is now quite certain that the Trog is gloriously insane.

After scraping his palms, turning his ankle and bumping his head more times than he cares to count, Callum finally feels a cool salty breeze on his face and, looking up, sees the Trog silhouetted against a shaft of daylight. Filled with an overwhelming sense of relief, Callum surges forward to join his saviour in the fresh air. He emerges, blinking, onto a rocky shelf at the base of a gannet-covered cliff, his senses filled with shrieking seabirds, sharp smells and the unfamiliar bright light. The sun has broken through during his spell in the cave, and it takes a full minute for his eyes to adjust.

When at last he can take in the scene around him, he is startled to see Things-of-Green grinning wickedly at him from a patch of thrift sprouting from the rocks. He is in his most impish form—pointed ears and ivy-leaf clothes—and the Trog is kneeling before him in worship, singing his ridiculous song in ever-more passionate tones. For some reason, the scene makes Callum angry, and he strides over to the two figures.

"What are you doing to him?" he demands of the grinning green figure. "Why is he kneeling to you?"

"This one *believes*," replies Things-of-Green simply. Callum is not impressed.

"Why should he kneel?" he demands again. For some reason he can't quite explain, he is disgusted that a man who has saved his life should be crawling around for Things-of-Green. The infuriating creature just smiles, spreads his arms and looks to the sky.

Now, although this bizarre beast still glows against the landscape with a weird, thrilling magic, Callum's anger won't let him be bewitched. He bends down next to the Trog and lays an arm over his shoulders.

"Are you okay?" he asks. The little man looks up, startled.

"Yes, yes, of course!" he chirrups, then, in a rather frightened voice, he asks, "Why do you not kneel?"

Callum almost laughs. "Um...I prefer to stand," he answers, not wishing to embarrass the little man. "By the way," he adds, "what were you singing?"

The Trog looks delighted by Callum's question and rises stiffly to his feet.

"Ah! The hymn! Look!" He reaches into the clarty folds of his fur cloak and pulls out an object: pale orange, cylindrical and faded. He holds it out to Callum on outstretched palms as if it is a holy relic. Callum gingerly picks it up and peers at it critically.

"What is it?" he asks. The Trog gets fidgety.

"A holy sign!" he gurgles. "A gift! A gift from the sea!"

Callum lifts it up and scrutinises it carefully. After about ten seconds, he recognises it as a spent distress flare, the kind of useless rubbish which is always washing up on the beach at Skerrils. He studies it, angry, unimpressed, and says sharply, "This isn't a gift! This is just litter!"

The Trog seems unfazed by this assessment and happily takes the flare back, tucking it out of sight in his strange clothes.

"Ah," he smiles, "*anything* can be a gift if you *understand*!"

For a brief second, Callum feels foolish for not seeing any value in the flare. This feeling is quickly overtaken by sheer, bone-weary tiredness, however, and with a gruff, "I'm going home now. Thanks again," he turns and heads off round the rugged coastline.

Walking

Truth be told, Callum is quite enjoying his bad mood. He's stomping over the rocks with vigour and muttering under his breath about crazy cavemen, treacherous friends and troublesome nature sprites. "Kneel?" he splutters in righteous fury. "Kneel? *Me*? You won't get *me* kneeling, *no* way! Not to Steven *or* Things-of-Green!" He half expects some new and dangerous obstacle to rise up from the rocks ahead, or to come gushing out of the sea to his right, and he's secretly looking forward to the chance to get crosser still.

But it doesn't work out like that. For one thing, Callum is on a part of the coast he's never been to before; he must have been swept right round the headland before he was hauled ashore by the Trog. The rocks here are crumbly, different from the solid black stone closer to home. He can't see MacArthur's Island either, which means he's a good few miles from home if he hugs the coast the whole way.

"Hmmm," he says, and he stops his angry striding for a moment of reflection. That's when he realises, with a happy, calm certainty, that there's a shortcut over the cliffs he'll have no trouble finding. He cranes his neck to look up at the route. It's a climb that no sane boy would even consider making: the cliff is about forty feet high and nearly vertical; even walking to its base makes little showers of pebbles cascade and clatter down.

Somehow, though, Callum can see a path up the cliff, with good, solid hand-holds amongst the crumbly gravel. It's as if they're glowing invitingly, tracing a zigzagging path to the top, and all anger clears from Callum's mind as he acknowledges that Things-of-Stone is helping him out. With a delighted grin, he places his hand on the first glowing stone and hauls himself up.

Sure enough, the rock holds, though several of its neighbours come unstuck and bounce merrily down towards the water. Untroubled, Callum continues, up and up, till he's amongst the nesting gannets and guillemots. The birds eye him agreeably as he passes but make no attempt to flee, and Callum's heart fills with the warm glow of fellowship. He greets the birds breathlessly as he climbs.

"Afternoon, Mrs. Kittiwake," he says, and, "Sorry to disturb you, Mr. Razorbill!" Each time, he has the clear sense that the birds understand, and one or two even reply in their own, shrill language. Callum glances over his shoulder at the sea spreading out behind him, and he knows exactly how the birds feel when they leap from their ledges, spread their wings and soar out over the wide, sparkling blue. He's casually aware of the ridiculous danger of his situation but he knows he has nothing to be afraid of, and happily climbs on.

At last, he crests the clifftop and flops down in the long grass, panting. The grass is still wet from the morning rain, tiny quivering droplets of silver clinging to each long strand, and Callum gazes into them, fascinated by the colours and reflections in each one. It is as if every droplet has captured the world in glittering stasis, the sky and the soil and the great living energy, and suddenly Callum himself seems to be drawn right inside, contained in one swirling droplet.

At the same time, he knows he is just lying in the grass, but through the light of the droplet he can look right down into the blade of grass, watch the busy, splendid processes in its cells. He sees water surging through channels too tiny to be imagined, long bejewelled chains of sugar shunting like train carriages from leaf to root; he feels the breath on his cheeks as the grass lazily exhales and pure, sweet oxygen surges out around him. He senses the summer sun strumming on the plant's machinery like a harpist at the strings, and he understands the sweet, clockwork order of everything, the perfect, timeless brilliance.

"We do not wish to frighten you, Callum Maxwell," says a voice inside it all, and Callum knows it is Things-of-Green. "We wish for you to enjoy the beauty. We need you to enjoy the beauty. That is all."

Gently, Callum's vision zooms back out and he sits up, a little dazed.

"I see it," he says. "If that's all you need, I see it." He gets to his feet a little shakily and looks out over the broad green field. He's never been here before but knows the way home as surely as if he had been at Papa's house. Smiling, he sets off, a skylark trilling and twittering above him, and he wonders if he was right to hear a note of apology in Things-of-Green's words.

Pushing on through the grass and bracken, Callum becomes aware he has a companion. It is Things-of-Blood, padding alongside in the guise of a friendly dog before getting up on his hind legs to take on a more human form. Callum walks on, glad of the company but feeling no real need to speak.

"It is not all we need," says Things-of-Blood as they carry on together.

"No?" asks Callum, only slightly interested. He is filled with a feeling of great well-being and doesn't really care about mystery anymore.

"Do you wonder how we do what we do?" asks the strange figure beside him. Callum shrugs.

"Magic, I suppose," he says.

Things-of-Blood laughs, a strange, rumbling laugh. "Magic is your name for the things of the world you do not understand," he says. "When you understand them, you call it science. But the things are just the things, whatever you choose to call them."

"Okay," says Callum, noticing with pleasure that he can see the tip of the monument peeping out from behind a foothill; he must only be a mile or so from home. "Well, you're sort of spirits, aren't you?" he says, then, feeling he should expand on this, he adds, "You're sort of, well, powerful spirity things. You can control stuff, like, well...like spirits," he finishes weakly.

"So," chuckles Things-of-Blood, "you think we are *spirits*! Well, no more than you are, Callum Maxwell, and no less. Did you say we were powerful?"

Callum is surprised by the question. It sounds like Things-of-Blood is digging for compliments.

"Well, let me think about that for a second," he says sarcastically. "You can make animals talk. You can make stone come to life. You can control the sea. You can show Craig some battle that happened hundreds of years ago. You can turn people into birds or let them breathe underwater. Yes, you know, I think that would count as being powerful!"

He glances at his companion, intrigued how he'll react to this witty response and is horrified to see that Things-of-Blood has undergone a startling change of appearance. He is still in human form, but he has shrunk almost to a skeleton. His skin is ashen grey, and his head is bald and speckled with unhealthy-looking blotches. He stares at Callum from dark, sunken eyes, making him stop dead in his tracks.

"*All for nothing*, Callum Maxwell," he rasps, his voice dry and distant. "All that is done can be *undone*. Power fades. Beauty fades. If you do not give us what we need, *He* will go and take all with him. *Believe*, Callum Maxwell!

"*BELIEVE!*"

And, reaching out one bony claw while clasping his throat with the other, Things-of-Blood collapses onto the ground and crumbles into a squirming mass of creeping, crawling things, worms and centipedes and caterpillars which disappear into the soil and undergrowth. Callum, with a shout of alarm and disgust, turns and sprints for Papa's house.

History 2

I don't get it!" says Callum, pacing up and down in Papa's front room.

It's the following morning, and Callum has not yet recovered. He didn't sleep well in the night and he's feeling crabbit. The fact that his mum has reminded him he has to go to the dentist in Glasgow this afternoon hasn't improved his mood either, so although he's gone round to Papa's to cheer himself up, it doesn't seem to be working yet.

"I mean, they're all saying it! '*Believe*!' Believe *what*? I don't *need* to believe now, do I? I *know* they exist. I've spoken to them all!"

Papa is watching Callum with a sympathetic eye, quietly filling his pipe for his first smoke of the day.

Callum goes on. "I mean, they've proved their point! Really! I'm not about to forget them now, am I?" He slumps into an armchair. "Wish I bloody could, actually!"

Papa frowns. "Language!" he warns, and Callum gives an apologetic smile. "Now look here, laddie, have a cup of tea till I tell you a wee story." He pours Callum a cup of tea and passes it to him. Callum leans over for the sugar bowl and ladles it in while Papa begins his story.

"Now, Callum. I told you last time that I had friends with me when I first met Things-of-Green, and so I did. There were three of us in the beginning. Elsa, your grandmother, got to know them later, as I've told you, but at first there was myself, Gordon MacQuarrie and Connor McKnight. We were great pals, you know—used to get up to all sorts of mischief. If the ghillie ever passed us in the street, he'd box our ears as a matter of principle. 'That's for all the things I never caught you for,' he'd say." Papa chuckles. "It was fair enough. We were always up on the estate, helping ourselves to birds' eggs, guddling for trout, hunting for rabbits."

Callum is taken aback. "You mean you were *poachers*?" Papa himself had been a ghillie for years and had always spoken of poaching as if it were a grave offence.

"Och, yes," replies Papa breezily, lighting his pipe with a flourish. "Not terribly good ones, mind you, but catching the animals was never really the point, you see. All we wanted to do was romp over the moor and have adventures." Papa's eyes take on a distant, dreamy look. "They were good times, Callum." He sighs.

Callum is impatient. "*And?*" he prompts, and Papa remembers himself.

"And," he says. "Yes, *and*, we thought we were quite the thing. We thought we knew that landscape like the backs of our hands.

"One day, though, we were getting up to our usual nonsense when we spotted a kind of grassy hummock on the mountainside that we'd never noticed before. We headed straight for it, thinking it would make a great lookout post when we needed to keep an eye out for the ghillie and his dogs. When we got to it, we were quite astonished to find there was an entrance to it. The neatest wee hidden entrance you could imagine, draped with ferns and only just big enough for us to crawl through, small as we were.

"I went in first. I was thinking it might be some kind of old burial chamber, you know, that there might be some treasure or something in there. I crawled through into the darkness, couldn't see a thing, but I could tell there was space inside for all three of us so I shouted the others to follow. Robert usually had some matches with him so I thought we'd be able to get some light and have a good poke around. I was thinking this was going to be the best den we'd ever had.

"Anyway, through they came. But before I could get Robert to strike a match, the whole chamber suddenly lit up with the strangest green glow. You couldn't tell where the light was coming from, but it filled every corner, and we could see we were in a sort of room. This was no natural cave, you understand. It had been carved and chiselled out of the rock. Smooth, flat floor, high walls, and the ceiling was curved—arched, you know, like in the kirk. And at one end, there was a broad, flat, table sort-of-thing. Like an altar, I suppose. And standing round it, perfectly calmly...well, you can guess!"

Callum is on the edge of his seat, tea forgotten and cooling in the cup.

"Things-of-Green!" he shouts.

Papa smiles. "Aye, Things-of-Green, and Things-of-Blood, Things-of-Stone and Things-of-Water. Just standing there, sort of fizzing away with energy, and the three of us were frozen to the spot. This was the first time, you see, the first time we met them. And they'd made an effort to impress, you know. They looked like four ancient warriors, gold torques around their necks, spears and armour and so on, but they were also doing that shifty, shimmering thing where they seem to be thousands of different shapes at once."

Callum nods. He knows exactly what Papa means.

"It was really very impressive! We knew we were seeing something deeply ancient, deeply powerful, deeply strange.

"And then Things-of-Green spoke to us. He said, 'What gifts do you bring?'" Papa runs a hand through his silvery hair, shaking his head with a disbelieving chuckle that sends wreaths of smoke into the room.

"Us! Three wee nyaffs from Skerrils! And these magical ancient beings are looking to us for some presents!

"Well, we had nothing for them, of course, which didn't seem to matter really. When we left the chamber, we found we'd been changed completely, could see things in the world that had been invisible to us before—just as you have yourself, Callum. And for the next few weeks we had adventures just as you've been having. They showed us things, took us off to their weird nether-land, and I could suddenly read the landscape just like a book. I've never looked back!" Papa smiles, but Callum isn't satisfied.

"But what's the point?" he asks impatiently. "I mean, that's all just more or less what's happened to me! What's it got to do with them telling me to believe all the time?"

Papa shifts in his chair. "The thing is, laddie, each of us reacted to this quite differently. We'd all had the same experience, but it affected us all in completely different ways.

"Gordon was really quite fleggit by it all. He was terrified. He started talking about them as if they were demons or evil spirits or something. I asked him why, and all he could tell me was he'd seen what they were *really* like, what they'd always been like. He said they wanted to be worshipped, wanted sacrifices and suchlike."

Callum is shocked. "But they don't," he protests. "Do they?"

Papa looks a little sheepish. "Well, they've never wanted any from *me*," he says. "You don't *need* to sacrifice goats to them or anything. The thing is, though...well, the thing is, they don't mind if you *do* go in for that sort of thing. I think, perhaps, it's the sort of thing they got used to in the old days, when everyone knew about them and felt the need to make offerings to them."

Callum is appalled. "That's awful! So they *are* evil, then?"

Papa looks at him sadly. "Och, son, it's nowhere near as simple as all that. They aren't really responsible for the way we react to them. They just need some kind of reaction! No, don't ask me why—I can't say I've ever figured it out. But while Gordon was getting more and more feart, Connor decided that he would follow these beings like a faithful dog. He started making up little ceremonies to please them. He'd bring his pocket money up to the hillside and bury it for them. It did no earthly good, of course, but they never tried to stop him."

"So what happened? Where are your friends now?"

Papa gives a sad smile. "Well, Gordon MacQuarrie finally decided to deny that he'd ever seen anything strange in the mountain that day. He said it was all wicked lies, that we were suffering from some kind of mania. He started going to the kirk every day while

Connor and myself were out on the hills. He stopped seeing us, wanted nothing to do with us. He wouldn't talk to us at school, and he even started warning other people against us. It wasn't funny."

"Wait a minute," gasps Callum. "Don't tell me Gordon MacQuarrie is *Mr.* MacQuarrie? He's not the minister, is he?"

Papa gives a solemn nod. "That's him," he says sadly. "He's been hiding from Things-of-Green and the others for over seventy years! I wish I could say it's made him happy, but, well...I don't think it has."

Callum thinks of the miserable, ancient figure who stalks through the town, scowling at any sign of merriment or humour. "No," he agrees, "I don't think so either." Then a thought strikes him. "What about your other friend? What about Connor? How is he?"

"Well," says Papa, "I'm not sure. You've seen him more recently than I have!"

Callum is confused for a second but then the penny drops.

"Not...not the *Trog*?"

Papa winces. "I wish you wouldn't call him that, Callum. It's not very respectful. But yes. That's Connor. Everything a ritual, everything a ceremony, trying to show them just how much he worships them. In his own way, he's as scared as Gordon."

Callum gives a shudder. The conversation has filled the room with a gloomy atmosphere, which is very unfamiliar, and Callum wants to return to the peace and comfort he expects from a visit to Papa's house.

"*You're* okay, though," he says. "Knowing about Things-of-Green didn't turn *you* crazy!"

Papa shrugs. "No, it didn't. Nor Elsa, when she got to know them. But that's the thing. They don't know how any of us will react to them. We bring ourselves to the meeting, if you see what I mean, and they're getting less and less familiar with the sorts of people we are now. People are changing, Callum, our connection to the land is nothing like what it once was. There's only a few of us left who can deal with it properly. I happened to be one of the lucky ones. I think you will be too. I'm not sure about your friends, though."

"But why bother, then? If it drives most of us insane, why do they keep interfering?"

"Because," says Papa in a low voice, "without us they are nothing. This is why they are getting more desperate, more extreme—you know, Steven's adventure with the selkies? Nothing like that happened to me or my friends. Their need is getting more urgent. They're revealing much more of themselves than they ever did to us."

"Papa," says Callum in a small, worried voice, "Things-of-Blood said something strange. He said, '*He* will go and take it all with him!' Who was he talking about?"

"That, my boy," replies the old man, "is something we must find out."

Dentist

It's with a busy head that Callum climbs into his mum's car that afternoon for the journey to Glasgow. He'd love more than anything to tell her about his adventures, to be able to hear a new point of view, but of course, he's still unable to speak of any of this to anyone who hasn't seen for themselves. Even if he had been able to, Mum is not the best conversationalist while driving.

It's a common problem for people who do most of their driving round tiny, single-track roads: the prospect of taking the car into a sprawling metropolis like Glasgow is one of the most stressful things they can imagine, worse than any expedition to the Amazon or Antarctica, and so Mum spends the journey tight-lipped and gripping the steering wheel so hard her knuckles are white. Since she seldom takes the car over forty miles per hour, Callum has plenty of time to look out the window at the passing countryside and ponder his current problem.

For the first thirty miles or so, the road out of Skerrils is winding and narrow, snaking through glens and over old stone bridges, rattling over cattle grids, through scattered patches of woodland and broad open moors. Although he has no great love of going to the dentist, Callum does enjoy the journey, and he's pleased to find that even through the window of a car, his newfound knowledge of the landscape is as real and present as ever. He looks up into the pale sky and sees a buzzard hovering over a field, and for a giddying instant, he can see the buzzard's point of view, feels himself searching the sedge for the scuttlings and rustles of some delicious rodent. Then they're round a bend and his view changes again.

This time, he gazes over vibrant green hills, and he can pick out a million subtle shades and variations in colour, see the racing shadows of clouds as giant, painterly strokes sweeping the land. Questions and doubts drift from his mind and he is free to simply enjoy the experience. Even his lingering dread about Steven's watery fate seems to lift, and he's able to wonder lazily how his friend is getting on in his underwater kingdom. He looks forward to telling Vicky and Craig about it when he gets home.

After a while, the road broadens, the speed picks up and they're passing more and more traffic. Two lanes become four, and Mum leans stiffly forward in her seat, staring ahead as if she's afraid to blink. She is not exactly relaxing company, and her stress is starting to affect Callum.

"Are you okay, Mum?"

"Fine," she says tersely.

"Do you want to play twenty questions?" he asks, thinking some distraction might do her good.

"Shoosh, Callum," she snaps, sitting even further forward and clutching the steering wheel for dear life.

Callum gives up and looks out the window again. His view of the landscape is now blocked by buildings. They are passing shopping centres, industrial estates, car parks. Road signs are huge and blue, not the rustic green of home, and Mum slows to a crawl at every one of them for fear of missing a single detail. She repeats them under her breath, terrified of leaving the road at the wrong point, but equally terrified of entering the city at all.

Mum and Dad love to share horror stories of trips to Glasgow cursed by wrong turns, hours spent trapped in the one-way system, helpless meanderings into neighbourhoods with boarded windows and graffiti on every wall. They speak of the city with a certain grim relish, as if reminding themselves of how dirty, ugly and dangerous it is somehow makes their lovely wee village all the more special and safe. This is all very well, until they actually have to *go* to Glasgow; then they become victims of their own imagination, certain anything that *can* go wrong is more or less guaranteed to do so.

Callum's never really minded the city. He's had to go quite regularly, ever since he broke a tooth falling out of a tree, and apart from the fact it turns his parents into gibbering wrecks, he's always found it to be quite exciting. He loves the bustle, the giant, red sandstone buildings, so much grander and more ornate than they need to be. The traffic and noise is all so different from home that it's exotic and intoxicating; back before Things-of-Green removed all trace of boredom from life at Skerrils, Callum sometimes wished he could live in a big city where things always seem to be *happening*.

Today, though, something is strange.

Mum has pulled off the motorway and they are descending into the city amidst a speeding tangle of roads, traffic zooming past them on all sides. A light smir is descending from low, grey clouds, and Mum is muttering in agitation. She puts on the windscreen wipers, much faster than they need to be, and they sweep frantically at the window.

This does nothing to calm Mum's nerves, and she flaps at the controls on the dash, accidentally turning on the indicators to the confusion of the driver behind, who toots his horn in annoyance. Mum slows way, way down, and cars speed past with angry faces glaring from inside. At last she pulls into a side street and stops, breathing hard.

None of this is unusual, however; this is the way they always make their entrance to the city. But something *is* odd. Something is not right.

Mum decides to ditch the car and walk to the hospital, so they step out into the grey day, zipping up their jackets and finding their bearings. Mum heads off purposefully up the street, and Callum follows, but he is confused and frightened because he has now realised what is wrong.

They are not here.

Things-of-Green is not here. None of them are here.

He walks after Mum. The sky is dull. The street is wet and grey. There is no view but buildings. Cars pass on the road, and people bump past on the pavement. Their faces are closed and unfriendly. The air is filled with mechanical noise and the smell of petrol. Callum searches frantically for some sign, some signal, but finds none.

He pauses for a moment, but Mum comes back to grab him by the wrist.

"Come *on*, we're *late*!" she hisses, and she drags him across the road and up the hill to the bleak, black hospital building. Crowds are surging down the road, blank-faced, unhappy crowds.

Callum is suddenly terrified, lost, disconnected. He's sure he can remember seeing green hills beyond the city in the past and he searches the horizon in desperation, but there is nothing beyond the blank buildings. Thick, leaden clouds have descended on the city, shrinking the world to these busy, unsympathetic streets. A fearful sob rises in Callum's throat as Mum pulls him through the glass doors and into the hospital.

They get into a lift. Silver doors close them in, and panic rises in Callum's chest. It's like being in prison, and Callum is howlingly homesick. He has never felt like this before. He starts to shake.

Mum, finally getting over the stress of driving, notices something's wrong. She gives Callum's hair a sympathetic ruffle. "Ach, c'mon, love," she says, "it's only the dentist!"

Callum is so overwhelmed he can't even tell her it's got nothing to do with the dentist. All he can do is look at her blankly.

The lift takes them to the fifth floor. As they step out, Callum hears the clanking gears and cables in the lift shaft and has the horrible feeling that they're in the middle of a giant machine. The doors slide shut behind them like the jaws of a hungry robot, and Callum's trembling gets worse. Nurses pad up and down the corridor; to Callum's mind, they're no more human than the gears and cogs of the lift.

"Callum, love," says Mum, real concern in her eyes now. "Come on, darling. This isn't like you!" But Mum's concern just throws the uncaring glances of the nurses into even sharper contrast.

Callum staggers through to the waiting room, clutching Mum's hand for support, but she lets go of him to register at the reception desk. He stumbles and falls onto the cold, polished floor, feels himself losing his grip on consciousness, being sucked into a dark, lonely void. The last thing he sees before he blacks out is a crumpled, broken fern, sprouting on the window ledge outside beyond two panes of dirty glass. There is no life in it, no thrumming, pulsing energy; only soot and filth and hopelessness, a dirty grey existence amidst dirty grey concrete.

"Skerrils," gasps Callum, and a cold darkness falls on him.

Home

Voices.

Bright lights.

A strange hubbub. Someone calling his name.

The sensation of rising up from out of deep water.

Callum opens his eyes and gasps for breath.

He's still in the dentist's waiting room, on the floor. He sits up.

Mum is there, and two nurses, who now look perfectly normal and human.

"I don't understand it," Mum is saying. "This isn't like him at all!"

One of the nurses is holding his hand, and the touch is warm and sympathetic. "You okay there, son?"

Callum's mouth is dry. "Um...yeah," he croaks. "I think so."

"What came over you?" asks Mum, gathering him up into an enormous hug. "You went out like a light! Are you ill?"

Another nurse arrives with a plastic cup of water, which she hands to him. "Sip this," she says, "you'll be fine!"

With a bit of effort, Callum manages to get up and walks with wobbly legs to a chair under the window. He glances out, looking for the fern, but he can't seem to find it. Other patients are watching him with kindly concern, and everything seems pretty normal.

"I'm fine," he says. "Sorry, Mum, I don't know what happened. I'm fine now, honestly!"

There are several more minutes of fussing before everyone seems satisfied that it was just a funny turn, and the nurses finally drift away, back to their duties. After a while, Callum is called in for his appointment, which is as uneventful as usual, and then they're back off out to the street and heading for the car.

Walking down Sauchiehall Street, Callum realises the clouds have lifted and he can now see beyond the city limits to the green hills of the north. There's still no sense of connection with the city around him, but at least he no longer feels as if he's going to be swallowed whole, that there's no escape. There *is* an escape. He can go home.

They get to the car at last, and Mum, who has been feeling Callum's forehead on and off throughout the walk, has now gone back into terrified-driver mode and seems to have forgotten Callum is even there. They manage to pull out into traffic, briefly career the wrong way up a one-way street, and leave the city heading south instead of west, but mistakes are soon corrected, and

Callum feels a great weight lifting from his shoulders as Glasgow finally disappears behind them.

He falls asleep on the drive home and doesn't wake up until they're practically back at Skerrils. As soon as the car stops, he leaps out, shouting, "I'm away to Vicky's house, bye!" before Mum even has time to protest.

"What about your tea?" she shouts after him, but Callum has far higher priorities right now than filling his belly. He urgently has to tell Vicky about his adventures, about what happened in Glasgow, and to find out what she thinks it all means.

He jogs up the road with a sense of such belonging and connection that he feels twenty feet tall. There is a broad grin on his face as he inhales lungfuls of sweet, clean air, every subtle scent of it another mark of home. Above him, the blue sky is crossed and recrossed by swallows and martins, and above them, swifts go shrieking after the high summer insects. The air is warm and still, and the sounds of the village hang lightly in it, as comforting and safe as a pair of bedroom curtains. Even the distant yapping of Mr. McKendrick's dog has its place, and Callum laughs at the bizarre memory of their first meeting with Things-of-Blood.

His smile is infectious, and everyone he passes returns it to him. Even though Callum knows his neighbours don't know, haven't met Things-of-Green and the others, he still feels warmly tied to each and every one of them. It's a comforting warmth—not as exciting or as electrifying as his new ties to grass and cloud and pebble and buzzard, but maybe none the worse for that.

In about five minutes, he's ringing Vicky's front doorbell. Vicky's mum Linda answers, looking vexed.

"Oh, it's you, Callum. Come in, son. Maybe you can talk some sense into her!" This is unexpected.

"Into Vicky?" asks Callum in surprise. "Why, what's wrong?"

Linda gives a gasp of frustration. "She's lost the plot, is what's wrong!" she exclaims, then, after a pause, "And I mean even more than usual! Come on through!"

Callum follows her through the narrow corridor, into the kitchen at the back where she lets him out through the back door into the garden. There, an unexpected sight meets his eyes.

Vicky, in her usual red T-shirt and brown cords, is stacking a giddying selection of musical instruments into a giant pile next to the dustbin. There's a banjo, two accordions of different sizes, a set of toy bagpipes, a guitar, dozens of flutes and whistles from exotic countries, a box of harmonicas in different keys, various drums, tambourines and cymbals, a saxophone, a harp, a thing he remembers Vicky calling a hammer dulcimer, and various other things for blowing, strumming, squeezing and hitting. Oh, and there's the cello, last spotted lying by the path up to the monument.

Callum's jaw drops. This *can't* be what it looks like.

"What...what are you *doing?*" he demands.

Vicky glances up, casually. "Oh, hi, Callum. Just having a tidy-up." She says it as if it's a pile of scrap paper and broken toys she's discarding, but the instruments in the pile tell the story of Vicky's whole musical life. These are the things she has loved more than anything. Every spare penny earned through odd-jobs and performances has gone into this collection. Every spare moment has been spent seeking out newer, more exciting and more challenging instruments. Sure, she's sometimes given away the odd recorder when she thinks she's mastered it, but there's always been the collection, the old friends she'll return to when she wants to make her brilliant, peculiar, wonderful music.

Callum is outraged.

"You *can't* throw this away!" he shouts. "It'd be like... it'd be like Papa throwing away his pipe, or...or Miss Duguid giving up the library, or Max giving up being a git, or...or... Actually, it's worse than *any* of that! What the heck are you *thinking?*"

Vicky just shrugs. "I'm finished with it," she says simply.

"But this is *you*, Vicky! This is *who you are!*"

For this first time, Vicky meets Callum's baffled stare, and he is immediately silenced by the look in her eyes. There is something deep going on in there; she hasn't made this decision lightly.

"Callum," she says quietly, "it's who I *was*. But how the heck can I go back to that after what we heard on the mountain? I mean, you were there! You think I can come near that with...with a bloody *trumpet?*" She spits the last word in contempt, rummages in the pile of instruments, pulls out a trumpet and bounces it off the wall in disgust.

"Language," Callum murmurs helplessly under his breath as the trumpet clatters to his feet.

"*Nothing* can come close to that, Callum. That was *it*. That was the *music*."

Her eyes are glistening now, and Callum can hardly bear to look at her, frightened that he'll burst into tears at what he's hearing.

She puts a hand on his shoulder. "It's okay," she says, though he can hear sadness in her voice. "I mean, who the heck gets to hear *that* in their lives? 'Course, it might have been nice..." She falters for a moment, looks at the instruments.

"What?" asks Callum. "What might have been nice?"

Vicky is silent for a little longer, then, after a deep, shuddering sigh, she looks at him and smiles. "It might have been nice to have a *bit* more time to look for it myself," she says. "But hey-ho. I'm sure something else will come along now."

And that's it. Her decision is final. And for the first time since their original encounter on the pebble beach, Callum wishes he could get his hands round Things-of-Green's scrawny, tangled twig of a neck and shake him senseless for what he's done to his friend.

MacQuarrie

The walk home has none of the pleasure of the walk to Vicky's house. The birds are still singing, the evening sun is still slanting over the rooftops of Skerrils, but the humming pulse of life beneath it all seems to mock Callum's every step. He half wants to stick his fingers in his ears, to shut his eyes—anything to drown it all out.

He sees a seagull hanging in the sky and finds himself blindingly aware of all of seagull-kind, the great feathery mass of them, their yearning for the wide wild sea and their frustrating need for land, one huge, swirling, beaky split-personality, and he shouts, "Och, can I not just see a *seagull* without it having to *mean* something?"

This draws a surprised look from a couple of passers-by, and in a front garden a man stops mowing his lawn to gaze at Callum in wonder. Too grumpy even to mouth a *sorry!* at them, Callum drives his hands into his pockets and stalks up the street.

Just then, he sees a figure up ahead, walking towards him, stopping, turning and hurrying away. Callum is surprised to recognise Craig, whom he hasn't seen for a couple of days. They have a *lot* of catching up to do— why is he running off?

"Oi!" yells Callum, breaking into a run. Craig casts a glance over his shoulder and speeds up. There's no doubt now; he's definitely trying to get away, but Callum's having none of that.

"*CRAIG*!" he bellows, putting on speed. There is absolutely no way, after everything, that *Craig* is getting to ignore him. I mean, come on. Callum is haring along now, slaloming through startled villagers, leaping over a dog's outstretched lead to a shower of excited yapping and an angry curse from the owner, gaining on Craig as he charges up the street. Craig is still running away, throwing fearful looks back at his pursuer, each of which makes Callum more and more determined to catch him.

At last, Craig ducks down the little side alley that leads to Gilmartin Street and is out of sight until Callum, breathless, reaches the corner and skids round it. He is just in time to see Craig disappearing into a dark little cottage through a black door. Callum is at the door in seconds flat, and through the last little gap he sees a black, shadowy figure and has the sense of his friend being engulfed in darkness.

"Craig!" he yells again, scared now. The door squeaks open a little, and out of the murk looms the crooked, joyless figure of Mr. MacQuarrie. His pale face wears a triumphant sneer and his dark eyes glisten.

"What is it that you're wanting here, young Maxwell?" he asks. His voice is dry, his skin the papery grey of a wasp's byke. His black clothes merge with the gloom of the house, so to Callum's distracted eyes he looks like a white head and a pair of bony hands floating, disembodied, in the darkness.

"I want my friend," says Callum, defiantly. "What's he doing here? What have you done to him?"

The sneer spreads further across the minister's face.

"You've no friends here, Maxwell," he gloats. "*We* know the sort of friends you keep. You and that grandfather of yours. There's *no place* for you here, amongst decent people!"

"This is rubbish!" snaps Callum, forgetting his manners in a way which would fair make his parents blush. "CRAIG!" he shouts, trying to penetrate the shadows beyond the minister's crooked frame. He makes to push past Mr. MacQuarrie, into the house, but the old man grasps his shoulder in a grip of surprising strength.

"I think not, boy," he says coldly, pushing Callum back into the alley hard enough to nearly cowp him.

Callum's birse is flying high now, and he's all set to force his way in, when a shrill voice comes from inside the house.

"Go away, Callum!" it shouts. "I don't want to see you anymore! Leave me alone!"

And suddenly it's not funny. All the fight goes out of Callum as the stark reality comes crashing in on him. That's another friend lost. Craig. Craig, who's been a pal since they both could walk, who's camped in his garden, walked the hills with him, swum in the sea and played football and fought and laughed and planned and played. Callum's shoulders slump, he hangs his head; he has no idea, for the moment, what to do next.

To his surprise, Mr. MacQuarrie steps forward and lays a sympathetic hand on his back. Callum looks up at the gaunt face, and it's no longer wearing the cruel sneer of before. In fact, there's something in the coal-black eyes that looks a lot like deep understanding.

"It needn't be like this, young Maxwell," he says. Callum is disarmed by a note of unexpected warmth in the old man's voice. "I understand what you're going through. I know the temptation that has been laid in your path." Craig has appeared at the door behind him, looking sheepish but expectant. The minister goes on. "You're young. Impressionable. It's no great sin that you should need wiser heads to guide you in testing times."

Craig steps forward. Inside Callum, a tiny wee voice is saying *listen to him! This could be the answer!*

"There are forces at work that are wrought of ancient evil." The voice is smooth, now, persuasive, and Callum is drawn to the idea of escape, a return to normality. "But you mustn't fear, boy. There is a greater power than these imps of temptation."

Imps of temptation—Callum quite likes that. He feels himself almost persuaded, almost yearning for a way out of all of this.

"A greater power which you will never know, stuck in the shadow of that wicked old man!"

It takes exactly three and a half seconds for Callum to realise this hideous old fossil is talking about Papa. As quick as a pistol shot, he is back in his own head, furious, bristling.

"I'll *wicked old man* YOU, you bony old bampot!" he bellows. "As for *you*," he adds, pointing an accusing finger at Craig, "away back to your silly video games, you big fat chicken! Reality too much for you, is it? Ha!" And he turns on his heel in disgust and stamps out the alley, back into the stretching sunlight of a Skerrils summer evening.

Or so he thinks, at first. But if you can imagine, for a moment, walking up a street that you've walked up a thousand times, a street in which every house, lamppost and paving stone is familiar—a street, in fact, that you know so well you don't even think about it as you walk along it. Imagine walking up such a street and then suddenly having the feeling that something is colossally, monumentally strange and wrong about it. This is the feeling that stops Callum mid-stride.

He looks around. Where is he?

At first glance, it still resembles the street he expects to see: High Street, the road to school, to Vicky's house, to the library. It's the same width. There are big, house-shaped things on either side, and tall, lamppost-shaped things sticking out of the ground. But as best Callum can recall, the actual houses on High Street never scowled at him in quite the way these giant, blocky objects are scowling. He's also pretty certain that the lampposts never had leaves sprouting out of them before and weren't made out of dark, thorny wood, either.

Looking down, the surface of the road, which should be new, smooth asphalt, now seems to be ancient cobbles sprouting with grass and thistles. Beetles scuttle around in the crevices between the stones, and worms writhe in the hollows of missing cobbles. If this is the result of some unexpected road redevelopment, Callum has to admit he preferred things the way they were before.

The final shock comes when, wishing to avoid the hostile stares of the hunching, house-shaped things which surround him, Callum looks ahead to see where this mysterious version of High Street leads. He is partially blinded by the giant setting sun, which hangs pinkly in the thickening air. Shielding his eyes, he sees this broken track no longer leads to anywhere he might want to be. Instead, it twists and winds its way up a grim, grey hillside, towards a forbidding tower of black rock. And silhouetted atop this tower, clearly visible in the sinking light, stand four terrible figures.

The light plays around them, like lightning flickering in the high clouds of a thunderstorm. Things-of-Green, Things-of-Stone, Things-of-Water and Things-of-Blood are wrapped in a terrifying majesty, and to Callum's knee-trembling consternation, they seem to be radiating a kind of ancient, towering rage. There is nothing small, nothing playful about them now. They are giant, they are powerful, and they are angry.

They are also, quite clearly, waiting for Callum.

"Okay," he says to himself in a trembling voice, "here we go!" And with a feeling in the pit of his stomach ten thousand times worse than being sent to the headmaster's office, he sets off along the trail to meet them.

Blame

The trail is terrible, and Callum has to pick his way gingerly over the broken stones to avoid turning an ankle or faceplanting in the weeds. At first, the difficulty is easy to ignore as his mind is fully occupied with fear, awe, amazement and several more of the major emotions. As time goes on, however, and he doesn't seem to be getting any nearer to the four grim figures on their tower of rock, other thoughts start to pop up in his head, thoughts like:

Actually, this is getting boring.

...and...

I'm really quite hungry now—I wish I'd had tea when Mum offered it!

His complaints and impatience start to overpower his fear, and he stops, puts his hand on his hips, and yells, "Look, if you want to talk to me, can't you just come down here?"

Before the words are even out of his mouth, Callum is lifted on a freezing blast of air and *scooshed* into the sky. He is now hurtling towards the tower, arms flailing and legs kicking and a loud and extremely rude word bursting from his lungs. He is aloft just long enough to see that the landscape he's flying over is, still, Skerrils, but a kind of nightmare Skerrils, where roads are black rivers, buildings are roiling, gurning giants, and the harbour is a wall of cruel, spiked rock battered by a howling, raging sea. He hasn't long to be properly terrified by this before he clatters, face first and winded, onto the top of the tower in the middle of the four terrible beings.

A fierce wind is howling round the tower so powerfully that Callum fears being blown to his death. Still, he struggles to his feet and braces himself against the gale. The moment he is upright, however, four thunderous voices bellow—

"*BOW!*"

—and the wind forces him to his knees.

Now, this is scary. In fact, it is downright blinking terrifying, and nothing in Callum's short life can possibly have prepared him for this. He really does think they're about to kill him, though he can't for a moment imagine why they would want to. A freezing tumult is pressing on him, and he finally senses these beings for what they are: ancient, pitiless forces of nature who have presided over the deaths of untold thousands—bird and beast, tree and shrub, hopeless women and powerless men—and Callum's sudden demise would mean as little to them as the crushing of a spider underfoot.

In this situation, you might imagine that now would be a good time to start doing what you are told. But, as you may have noticed, our Callum just isn't made like that.

Gritting his teeth and balling his fists, he pushes himself back to his feet and stands, tiny but defiant, in the full glare of the creatures' otherworldly eyes.

"*Why*?" he demands.

In an instant, the wind disappears, and Callum is bathed in warm, welcoming sunlight. The tower has become a green hill speckled with dazzling flowers. The air is thick with their sweet scent, and the four giant beings around him seem to speak of a million new beginnings, of births, of shoots thrusting through rich soil, of clean, clear rain washing all that is old and finished from the landscape. Callum is almost choked by the beauty of it, and he feels monumentally loved and precious, someone whose slightest hurt is a tragedy of universal significance. He falls over.

"Bow?"

This time, the word comes as a sweet suggestion, the warm request of a deep and trusted friend. And I mean, why wouldn't you bow? What is a little bow, after all, if it'll make your friends happy? If that's all they want, surely it's only polite.

But Callum isn't fooled. Laughing, now, and certainly impressed by the display, he'll still not bend the knee to anyone. Up he gets, back on his feet, and looks the four figures up and down.

"I'm sorry," he says, and means it, "but I'm not going to bow!"

Things-of-Green and the others are now shrunk to human form, more like the mischievous sprites with whom Callum was first acquainted. They move towards him like a small group of playground pals—weird pals, yes, but most of Callum's pals are weird—and they sit down on the warm grass. Callum joins them.

"Look," he says, "do you not think it's about time you told me what this is all about?"

Things-of-Green looks at him rather awkwardly, while the other three clear their throats, embarrassed, and look away. There's almost nothing odd about Things-of-Green now; this is the most human Callum has ever seen him. When he speaks, he even sounds like a wee boy.

"Um, yeah, sure," he says. "The thing is, Callum, and don't get angry when I say this. The thing is, you've sort of, y'know, failed?"

Callum is so taken aback by the chatty language that it takes him a moment to realise what has been said. When he does realise, he is very upset.

"What do you mean?" he demands. "Failed at what?"

Things-of-Green looks at Things-of-Blood as if asking for help.

"Well," says Things-of-Blood, "it's the whole belief thing, you know? We kind of needed you to believe in us? *Properly* believe in us, like?"

"I *do*, though," protests Callum, ignoring for the moment the fact that these almighty beings are blethering away like twenty-first-century kids. "For goodness' sake, how could I be having a conversation with something I don't believe in? Just because I don't want to *worship* you doesn't mean I don't think you're real!"

"Sure, sure," says Things-of-Green, "but, like, that's the whole problem? We kind of, like, *need* people to worship us? We're *supposed* to get folk to do it. If we can't manage that, then *He* gets angry."

"Put it like this," says Things-of-Stone. "If we don't have enough people impressed with what we do, then *He* thinks we're not working hard enough. Well, we *think* He thinks that, anyway."

Callum is getting exasperated. "*WHO?*" he shouts. "Who is *HE?*"

All four creatures look at him in surprise.

"The *Mountain*, of course!" they say in unison.

"The boss-man!" says Things-of-Green.

"The all-powerful!" adds Things-of-Water.

"His most glorious majesty!" puts in Things-of-Blood.

"The lord and master!" says Things-of-Stone.

"The *Spirit of Skerrils*!" they all finish together, and suddenly all four of them are grovelling on the ground, chanting in strange, ancient languages far older than Gaelic, performing weird signs and rituals in the direction of the mountain which remind Callum for all the world of the Trog's ridiculous songs and ceremonies in his dingy wee cave. He is completely banjaxed by all this.

"But... But... But I thought *you* were the Spirits of Skerrils," he stammers. "Sort of, anyway!"

They stop their shenanigans and turn to Callum again.

"We are," says Things-of-Green. "We have many parts! Each of us is but one aspect."

"But you're *ridiculously* powerful!" shouts Callum. "I've seen you do impossible things, *mental* things. I thought you could pretty well control the world if you wanted!"

Things-of-Blood looks at him sadly, and Callum once again sees the strain of ages upon them. No more childish banter, then.

"And yet," says Things-of-Blood, "you won't worship us, and you cannot keep your friends onside. The female cannot think of us more, the dark-haired one has joined your grandfather's old friend in foolish denial, and the underwater one...well, he was too easy! Only *you* know us, Callum Maxwell, and it is not enough."

"However powerful you think us, Callum Maxwell," says Things-of-Green, "there are always those *more* powerful. We are but part. The *Mountain* is the whole!"

Callum looks over to the mountain. It looms over the strange, dreamlike Skerrils, as dark and solid as it seems in his own world, and he has the strange sense of it having loomed over an infinite number of different Skerrils. It has been the backdrop to his whole life. He has seen the mountain in many moods—golden in a summer sunset, black against a starlit sky, threatening as it gathers the thunderclouds around its great rocky shoulders.

Always there, so big and so ancient, and Callum realises that it is *too* big to think of, really, and that most of the time the mountain is practically invisible to him and his friends. It's so much easier to take in the monument hill or to look out across the bay to MacArthur's Island. Even climbing the mountain only reveals a tiny fraction of its vast, rocky majesty. And he can almost, *almost* imagine it as a living presence of vast, unknowable power, holding the whole of Skerrils in its giant, ancient grip.

His thoughts are interrupted by a sudden question, however.

"What about Papa?" he demands. "*He* knows you just like I do! How many people do you need, after all?"

"Ahh," says Things-of-Blood, "your grandfather is indeed an old friend. But you creatures—you are so fleeting. So very, very fleeting. We needed *new* friends, now. Look." He points a finger down towards Skerrils, where the roads and streets are still crazy caricatures of the town that Callum knows, but recognisable all the same.

As Callum follows Things-of-Blood's gaze, he sees movement down there. Something is coming into the village from the road through the hills, something ugly and troubling. It creeps down the track that would be High Street in Callum's Skerrils, its movements alien and threatening, furtive, secret, dangerous. Callum feels a sudden surge of nausea when he realises it is a kind of giant insect, like a beetle or a cockroach, scuttling hungrily down the track, leaving a trail of filth and glaur behind it. Callum thinks he's going to boak.

A sound reaches him from below, a kind of wailing, shrieking howl. It's coming from this hideous creature, and Callum's horrified. What on earth is it? What does it want? And why do its sickening investigations seem to be taking it closer to the part of town where Papa lives?

A sudden fear rises in Callum's chest. "Take me back!" he yells. "Quickly! Please! Take me back to *my* Skerrils! Something's wrong! I need to go back!"

The air is filled now with the wailing of the loathsome creature, which flashes in different colours—blood red, the blue of frozen meat—all the while moving relentlessly on its scuttly legs towards Gilmartin Street and Papa's house.

"*Please*!" Callum shrieks, leaping to his feet and running down the hillside towards the town. As he charges, the four weird figures disappearing behind him, the landscape starts to change. The cobbled track turns back to a road, the truculent giants turn back into shops and houses, Skerrils re-forms itself as the village he calls home, and the hideous, ravening insect transforms into something far worse. It is an ambulance, and it is stopping outside Papa's cottage.

Departures

Callum runs with every ounce of his strength, all thought of his recent adventure gone from his mind, overwhelmed by fear for his Papa. *No, no, no, no, no, no, no, no, no, no,* is all that runs through his head. *No, Papa can't be ill. Papa's strong!* On he runs, trainers pounding the tarmac, wind streaming through his hair, stinging tears streaming from his eyes.

When he skids round the corner into Gilmartin Street, there is a small crowd gathered by the ambulance, worried glances passed one to another, low voices fearing the worst. A paramedic is politely but firmly moving people away from Papa's front door as his colleague pushes a stretcher into the cottage. Callum's mum and dad are there, and as soon as they spot Callum, they run towards him, Dad scooping him up in a hug and Mum trying to look brave, and failing.

Callum, utterly exhausted as he is, fights against his dad's embrace, shouting, "Let me go! Put me down! What's wrong with Papa?"

"Shoosh, son, shoosh," says Dad. "It's going to be okay. It's going to be okay, Callum!"

Callum wriggles free and runs to the door of Papa's cottage. "Papa!"

People in the crowd try to hold him back, but he pushes through, rushing into the front room where a terrible sight meets his eyes. There is a figure lying on the carpet, an old, frail figure without a hint of life about it. There is a plastic mask over its face attached to some sort of air tank, and its shirt is pulled up as a paramedic places the paddles of a defibrillator to its chest. The other paramedic notices Callum's arrival and says something, but Callum can't hear it over the high-pitched squeal of the machine. There is a loud crack, the figure jolts, and both paramedics lift it onto the waiting stretcher.

A part of Callum knows the figure is Papa, but for some reason he still finds himself looking around the room to try and find him. The stretcher is pushed past, and Callum is hustled out of the way by one of the paramedics, and someone from the crowd has come in to try and talk to him, but nothing is really making sense. Papa would be able to tell him exactly what's going on. Callum desperately wants to talk to him. What is this strange object being wheeled out of the cottage, lifted into the back of the ambulance?

This tiny, waif-like figure, obscured by wires and tubes, being fussed over by strangers?

Mum and Dad have made it to the cottage and are trying to talk to Callum. Dad says something about a heart attack, but he's pretending to be hopeful.

"They say there's a pulse, Callum, they're going to do everything they can," he says. Mum is giving him a watery smile, saying she'll go with Papa, make sure he's okay. Callum knows they're trying to comfort him but he feels completely, hopelessly alone, and without being able to answer them, he goes back into the front room and sits in his usual chair. He's never been in here alone before, and he's oddly fascinated by the strangeness of it.

Outside, Mum has clambered into the back of the ambulance and it pulls away, speeding off towards Glasgow with a flash and a howl as the crowd slowly disperses. One or two people glance in the window at the wee boy sitting on his own, but they're good folk and they don't disturb him.

Callum listens to the clock ticking and looks around the sparse little room. There are a few books: some poetry, some stuff about fishing, a novel or two. There's a framed photo of Papa proudly holding an enormous salmon, and another black-and-white photo of Papa and his wife, whom Callum never met. They have the strange, old-young look of people in faded photos, and

Callum is suddenly overwhelmed with the horrifying truth of it: Papa is very, very old. Old people don't last forever.

Papa might be gone.

Callum looks at his empty chair, feeling numb. He should be reacting, but nothing seems to come. It's not until he notices Papa's pipe, lying cold and empty on the sideboard, that he bursts into bitter, wracking tears. Every image of Papa that comes to his mind sets off a fresh wave—early memories of sunlit walks, riding on Papa's shoulders, listening to his stories out on the open moor. Papa, always there, always welcoming. And more recently, the cottage as the safest, happiest place in town, hot tea and long blethers, the only place where Callum has felt that the crazy wild magic of recent weeks might make some kind of sense.

The sobbing fit lasts for several minutes, and at the end of it Callum feels as empty as the room he is sitting in. He wipes his eyes with his sleeve, gives a final sniffle and stands up. It's only then he discovers Dad has been waiting at the door for him, quietly giving him the time he needs.

"Come on, son," says Dad kindly, and they step outside, shut the cottage door behind them and set off towards home. The sun is low on the horizon now, and the town is soft and quiet in the gloaming. "He'll be getting the best care he can, you know," Dad is saying.

Callum is trying to believe him, but there's something distracting him. Up ahead, in the road, a fair number of the crowd who had been gathered at Papa's front door are now standing in the middle of the road, gawping at something Callum can't see.

Dad is irritated; he doesn't want any distraction from the important business of comforting Callum. "Tsk. What now?" he mutters under his breath.

They're nearly with the crowd, close enough to hear a general rising murmur of surprise and shock. Callum recognises Dr. Harrison amongst them and is thinking of asking her what's going on, when she suddenly ducks as a crow comes shooting up the street towards her.

The crow wheels round and heads off towards the mountain, and suddenly the crowd is shrieking and leaping around as mice, rats, squirrels and birds come surging through them in a panic. All round the town, dogs are howling and cats claw at windows to get out.

Dad shouts in consternation and tries to pull Callum away, but he presses forward, through the frantic crowd and the fleeing animals until he can see, at the very centre of the commotion, a bizarre, ancient figure making his way purposefully up the High Street towards him. The figure is dressed in animal skins and rags and is surrounded by a scurrying, skiltering flight of creatures. Amidst the shrieks and cries of the fleeing crowd, Callum recognises this uncanny individual.

It is Papa's old friend, Connor McKnight, known to generations of Skerrils school kids as *The Trog*. And he is marching towards Callum with a purposeful stride, shouting something in his strange, cracked voice.

"It is happening!" he shouts, pointing a bony hand at Callum.

"Come away, Callum!" shouts Dad, trying to hustle him through the stramash and back towards home, but Callum is rooted to the spot. The Trog is almost upon them now.

"It is happening!" he quavers again, and Callum is horrified to see tears streaming down the old man's cheeks.

"What?" asks Callum in a whisper. "What's happening?" He already knows the answer.

"*Look*!" hisses the Trog, pointing towards the looming presence of the mountain. "*Look*!

"*He* is leaving!"

Mountain

A nd suddenly it is silent. The street, the town, is totally deserted, and the unexpected stillness rages in Callum's ears far more threateningly than the screams and bellows of a moment before. All around him, hanging in the air, is a terrible sense of loss and dread, and although the fleeing animals have now vanished, Callum is filled with their panic and he wants nothing more than to turn and run. He can't, though. He is frozen to the spot, paralysed. The Mountain is behind him and he wants to turn and look, but he can't. What will it look like? How can a mountain leave?

It is not only Callum who is paralysed. Skerrils is in stasis. Not a shadow moves; not a curtain flutters. No ant parades across the pavement; no gull slides across the sky. There is no whisper of sound from the sea, no rustle of wind in the leaves. Everything, everything is waiting. Callum doesn't know what it is they're waiting for, but he knows it isn't good.

Then it begins. Slowly at first, so that Callum isn't sure it's not just his eyes playing tricks on him, but there is movement down there at the bottom of the road, approaching from the sea. Something is sliding through the town, slowly, uncertainly, like spreading frost on a pane of glass. Callum looks from left to right, and the effect, whatever it is, is not just affecting the town. This sinister, slow, creeping thing is spread from horizon to horizon, a rising, relentless tide.

It is now close enough for Callum to try to figure it out. It isn't a shadow or a rolling haar, though it has something of those about it. It is not filling the space as it comes towards him, it's, it's...

And then he has it. It is an emptying. A draining, sucking loss. Where he stands, Skerrils is still alive and connected, but down beyond this spreading line of change, there is a shrivelling, severing, shattering of connections, a snapping and a twanging as rock and street and grass and hill collapse into a desperate solitude, a crumbling, colourless isolation.

Then, through the held-breath atmosphere, comes a terrible, trumpeting din, and Callum, to his horror, recognises the song of the Mountain hideously distorted. No longer the soul-soaring beauty he shared with Vicky, it sounds like the death throes of some almighty beast combined with the shattering screeching cacophony of a catastrophic train crash, and he is finally released from his paralysis and able to turn, cry and sprint for the Mountain. He doesn't know what he plans to do, but he knows he must do *something*, and he knows he must run for his life and for the lives of all he loves.

Off up the street past the old folks' home, onto the mountain path, the all-consuming emptiness chews at his heels. He throws a terrified look over his shoulder and sees MacArthur's Island as grey and flat as a clumsy drawing. All colour is being mercilessly pulled away from the landscape like a warm sheet pulled from a bed on an icy morning. What makes it all the more painful is that the landscape he is coursing through hasn't lost it all yet, but the warm attention he has felt since his first meeting with Things-of-Green now feels like a desperate plea for assistance. It's as if every pulsing cell in every single living thing is aware its moments are numbered, and it makes the impossible beauty of it both piercingly precious and desperately painful.

"What can I do, what can I do?" pants Callum as he charges on, terror at his heels and his whole head ringing with the Mountain's lament. Perhaps it is his pounding feet, but as he looks up the track ahead towards the mighty peak, it seems as if everything is shaking, vibrating, shuddering, and the light is fading around the edges, his vision growing dim.

Everything is leaving.

Skerrils is going to lose everything. And there is nothing to do but run.

In the lowering darkness, in the rising chill, Callum becomes aware that he is not alone. Although he is powering along at full tilt, four familiar figures are keeping pace with him, though they seem to be moving in slow, ponderous steps. To Callum's left, Things-of-Green and Things-of-Blood; to his right, Things-of-Water and Things-of-Stone. They are giant, luminous and cold, and they stride alongside him without giving him a glance. Each seems alien and distant, inhuman, remote. Their eyes are fixed ahead, their long legs sweeping through the heather, their arms swinging stiffly as they march. They cast no backwards glance at Skerrils, at the home they have transformed so dazzlingly for Callum. If they ever truly cared about it, that care is passing with the Mountain.

"Hey!" shouts Callum. "HEY!"

It's all he can manage. It is not enough.

And now it is upon him.

As the four emotionless figures stalk on, Callum's strength leaves with them, and he stumbles onto the rocky path, just as the nauseating wave of loss finally catches up with him.

The shaking landscape grows still and cold, and whatever it was that filled his world with light and hope, hilarity and love, is gone. Callum crumples in on himself and weeps in frustration. He is furious.

This is *his* fault. He could have stopped this. But now it's too late.

For five long minutes, he lies where he's landed, too weak to stir, too tired to try. At last, however, he realises it's getting properly cold, and the sweat from his frantic flight is cooling quickly on his skin. He begins to shiver and decides it's time to get back home, or to whatever's left of it. So he stands up.

He daren't look at the Mountain, so he turns towards the town and takes a step. The crunch of his foot on the gravel sounds dull and dead, and it's in danger of sapping the little motivation he has. He doesn't want to go home. He doesn't want to feel the emptiness, to look at the trees and see only trees, to look at the stones and see only stones. Worst of all, he is scared of what he'll see when he meets his friends and family. Will he be able to talk to them about it? Will they share his howling loss? Will they even *notice* that everything, everything is different...is worse?

Another reluctant step. His breath hangs in the cold, dull air. He's freezing now, teeth chattering and knees knocking, and he has to get home if only to avoid dying of hypothermia. He screws up his resolve and continues. This is going to be awful. Skerrils is going to be cold and blank and dead, like, well, like Glasgow was earlier that day. Callum gives a choking laugh—is it really still the same day? It feels like a lifetime ago.

But as he walks and ponders, something tickles the back of his mind. *Glasgow.* He never had the chance to talk to anyone about that weird experience, and now the only person who might have been able to explain has gone there himself. What exactly *did* happen? And why did it stop after he fainted?

He thinks back. The feeling of disconnection, the feeling that the place had no heart—was that *real?* There was the fern on the windowsill, the cold, isolated, little fern, but when Callum woke up, it wasn't there. Did he imagine it all? Had it just been some sort of *trick?* Why had he been so willing to forget all the real excitement and wonder of past visits to the great sprawling city?

Glasgow. Where Papa is. Callum walks on. *Where they are taking care of him.* Callum walks on. *Where strangers care in giant, towering buildings, where good people are working and sweating and dashing to and fro to save the life of one old man they have never met before.* Callum walks on.

Where power pulses through wires from distant stations, carried over hill and glen at impossible speed just so these good people can see enough to save him, so their machines, invented by long-dead geniuses for the good of the world, can do their work and save him. Where things of wire and things of glass and things of concrete and plastic and oil are rushed from floor to floor to save him...

Where roads will carry Callum to his side inside the speeding shell of the family car, helped and protected by a giant spreading system which wants only for a family to be safely reunited. And Callum is *there*, suddenly right there, in the ward with Papa and the surging teeming team of experts who are *willing* the life back into those precious old bones, doing what Things-of-Green and the others couldn't even begin to comprehend, and Callum *is* the doctor, and Callum *is* the surgeon, and the nurses and the cleaners and the receptionists and the cooks, and Callum is Papa, lying there on the edge of life and death—

And then Callum is Callum, turned and sprinting furiously back up the dark mountain path and screaming, *"Wait*! *This is WRONG! WAAAIIIIIIT*!!

"You DON'T need us to believe in you! You DON'T need our worship!

"It's YOU!

"YOU need to believe in US!"

Interlude

Suddenly
lots of things
start to happen
violently, all at once

Callum
is lifted up
high into a raging,
burning, seething sky

Below,
the world
shatters like
a fallen mirror

Light
comes pulsing
from above, below,
from heaven and the earth

Sounds—
laughter, tears
the clash of steel
a rising, old, sad song

Time
is wheeling
backwards and
forwards and back

Things
done are undone
wishes made are unmade
those who have left, return

People,
marching people
from cave to hut to house
to clockwork perfect green grey cities

Cells,
of roses
of fleet-footed hare
of oak and ash, salmon and eagle

Split,
copy, split
multiply, grow
and die and grow and die

Callum
is nowhere
and Callum is everywhere,
everywhere, everywhere together

All
is magic
and all is true
and all is magic and true

And...

Stop.

Three Days Later

A fine mist sits over Skerrils in a sparkling summer dawn. It holds the light in a soft swirl; sounds, too, hang longer in its hazy grasp. Birdsong comes from some unknown corner and lingers sweetly, and the soft *shoosh* of sea on shingle reaches all the way to Callum's bedroom window. Skerrils is not awake yet, but Callum stirs in his sleep, mutters something and rolls over.

Not the most exciting bit of news, perhaps, but if you look closely through the curtain-drawn gloom, you'll see Mum, who has been dozing in a chair at his bedside, suddenly sits up, alert. She peers at Callum, who mumbles again, then she's up and tiptoeing urgently through to Dad. Dad is snoring softly away, but Mum gives him a shoogle and he opens his eyes blearily.

"Whumph?" he asks, cleverly.

"He's waking up!" whispers Mum, a tremble of excitement in her voice.

This is enough to pull Dad back to full wakefulness and he sits up, rubbing his eyes. "Are you sure?"

"Yes! Well, I think so. He's fidgeting and mumbling. Come on! But *be quiet*!"

The pair of them creep back into Callum's room and stand, holding each other, at his bedside. He's completely still.

"Are you *sure* you didn't dream it?" whispers Dad. "You've not had much sleep since, well, you know..."

Then Callum's voice comes peevishly through the half-light.

"Oh, *gie's peace*!" he grumbles, before rolling over and drifting back to sleep.

So of course, he doesn't see Mum and Dad hugging each other in delight and attempting the tricky task of performing a rapturous jig without making any noise.

*   *   *

Three hours later, Callum sits up in bed in doddery confusion. He feels wonderfully rested, peaceful and calm, but there's something peculiar about the day. He has a sense of a storm avoided, of trouble sorted out, of difficulties past, but he can't say how or why. He also feels that he's missed something, somehow, as if he's been away for a long, long time to some strange, distant place. He tries to grasp the feeling, but it's fading like a dream.

That's all strange enough, but he's also just a wee bit surprised to find Mum, Dad, Steven, Craig, Vicky and about six other people all crowded round the bed and staring at him with big silly grins on their faces. As he blinks around them, a great cheer goes up, and Vicky leaps onto the bed to give him such a hug that the wind is squeezed from his lungs.

"Callum!" she cries. "You're awake!"

Callum, spluttering from the force of Vicky's uncharacteristic affection, gazes at his audience with the strong suspicion they've all gone mad.

"Aye, well," he protests, "it's a bit hard to sleep when half the town is standing in your bedroom!"

Vicky hops off the bed, grinning, and Mum steps forward to take her place.

"Oh, son," she says, happy tears streaming down her cheeks. "You've not found it hard for the last three days! You've been out cold since the night of the storm!"

"What?" Callum is aghast. "What storm?" The gathered crowd are smiling at him sympathetically, and it's beginning to get on Callum's wick. "Mum, *what storm*?" he insists.

"You know fine," says Craig, encouragingly. "The *storm*! The night your Papa took ill and you went rushing off up the—"

"Papa!" shouts Callum, suddenly remembering. He struggles to throw the duvet aside and get out of bed, but with Mum still sitting on it, that is easier said than done. "Where is he? Is he okay?"

"Shoosh, Callum, shoosh," says Dad soothingly. "He's going to be fine. It was a bit of a fright, right enough, but he's made a fantastic recovery. In fact, he's coming home this afternoon!"

Callum sinks back down on his pillow, relief rushing over him like the bubbles in a Jacuzzi.

"Thank you," he whispers, looking at the ceiling and not really knowing who he's talking to.

A wee while later, once most of the well-wishers have left and Callum's managed to get up and dressed, he's sitting at the breakfast table with his friends. He's absolutely ravenous, and Mum has made him soft-boiled eggs with a mountain of buttered toast, which he'd be enjoying even more if Vicky, Craig and Steven didn't keep helping themselves to big swedges of it without asking. Amidst the cheery banter of the reunion, Callum tries to wheedle as much information out of his friends as he can, but before they can say very much, Mum has hustled them out, explaining that Callum needs his rest.

"Och, *Mum*!" he protests, but she's having none of it.

"Out!" she chides, and Vicky and the others head laughingly for the door, promising to have a proper catch-up later on.

Callum would quite like some time alone to ponder things. He has the niggling feeling that something doesn't make sense—that it's odd that Vicky, Craig and Steven are all together, as if there's some reason they should be missing, or arguing or, or...

Frustratingly, it seems Mum has no plans to leave him to his thoughts.

"Now then, mister." She smiles, sitting down at the table with him. "I imagine there are a few things you'd like to talk about!"

She gives him a squeeze, and a kiss on the forehead, and Callum pretends to object. He knows she means well, and he is feeling very well looked after, but his fuzzy mind reminds him Mum won't be able to talk about the things he wants to talk about. *She doesn't know about Things-of... That is, she's never met Things-of... Or Things-of...* Callum shakes his head. Why can't he finish the thought?

He shrugs it off, and tries for safer territory.

"Mum, tell me about the storm," he says. She ruffles his hair.

"Ah, yes," she says, "the storm. That was scary. You running off into the wild night, away up the path, and us still fretting over your Papa. Really, Callum, your timing was a bit off!"

"Aye," says Callum impatiently. "But *what happened*?"

Mum gives him a funny look. "Well," she says, "you did it, didn't you?"

"Did *what*?"

"You saved us. You stopped the Mountain from leaving!"

Callum nearly falls out his chair.

"I *what*?" Mum can't know about this, can she?

"The Mountain, Callum. The spirit of the Mountain. You made it stay."

"But... You mean... You *know* about all this?" Callum shakes his head, pinching himself to see if he really is awake.

"Know about all what?"

"The spirits! The Mountain! Things-of... Things-of..." But again, there's something in the way, something missing. Callum racks his brain to try and complete the thought, but he can't. *There were creatures. There were strange, powerful... Weren't there?*

"Callum, of course I know!" says Mum, a note of exasperation in her voice. "I mean, I could hardly miss the *Mountain*, could I? It's big enough, after all!" Callum is utterly bewildered.

"Does everyone know, then?" he asks.

"I should think so," says Mum, chuckling. "Honestly, Callum, what's the problem? It's okay. You did it. Skerrils is safe!"

Well, Callum's head is just birling and he needs some fresh air. He excuses himself from Mum, who urges him to take it easy, and steps out into the golden morning. The mist has lifted and it's already warm, even though it's not yet nine. He wanders up the road, fairly aimless, trying to sort out his thoughts.

Miss Duguid passes on her way to the library.

"Callum!" she shouts, delighted. "You're up and about! Good to see you. Oh, and well done with that Mountain! Don't know what we'd have done without you!" She hurries on before Callum can respond and he's left standing in the middle of the road, scratching his head in total confusion. Does *everyone* know about this now?

Carrying on, he passes a few more well-wishers, and sure enough each of them make some mention of the Mountain, talks to him as if he's achieved something fantastic. The only person who doesn't congratulate him is Max, who, on spotting Callum walking towards him, has turned around and fled.

That's weird, thinks Callum, but then he thinks he should be able to remember why Max is suddenly scared of him. *It's something to do with... With Things-of...*

Ach! It's absolutely maddening, like an itch you can't reach, or a face that looks familiar but you can't say where from.

Callum finds his course is taking him to the harbour, and he hears music coming from up ahead. A merry, skirling tune, expertly plucked from a guitar or a banjo or something, and he knows only one person who can play like that.

Sure enough, sitting on the harbour wall is Vicky, completely in a world of her own as she plucks and strums away at a battered old banjo.

Spirits lifted, Callum goes and sits beside her. She doesn't even acknowledge him until the tune's finished, then she turns to him and grins. "What do you think? Three pound fifty from the charity shop!"

"Great!" says Callum. Then a thought crosses his mind. "Hey, wait a minute. I thought you'd decided... Didn't you throw away—"

Vicky interrupts him. "Don't talk about it, Callum. I was wrong." She shrugs. "I can't really explain it. It all seemed very important at the time, but now... I mean, why on earth would I stop playing?"

Callum is delighted that Vicky seems back to normal, but there's definitely something very strange afoot. "Vicky," he says, "do you not feel like we're missing something? Like something important happened, and we've forgotten about it?"

Vicky looks at him piercingly. "Well," she says, "I sort of know what you mean. But I can't see what could possibly be more important than you keeping the Mountain where it belongs!"

Callum turns and looks at the Mountain. There it is, as always, solid and certain and strangely comfortable, and still too big to really think about. Everything is as it should be, isn't it? Skerrils is safe. The thought keeps bouncing round his head. *Skerrils is safe. And yet...*

"Come on," says Vicky, "Steven's getting some stuff together to build another boat!" And she's off, banjo slung over her shoulder, whistling a joyful tune.

Steven... Another boat...

"Wait for me!" shouts Callum, and he runs after her.

Ten minutes later, they're by Steven's side on the shingle beach. Craig is there already, happily helping Steven look for wood in the flotsam and jetsam of the tideline.

"Callum!" they both shout in delight.

"Just in time!" says Steven. "Look at all this stuff!"

Callum looks. They have gathered an impressive pile of wood: sticks and planks and bits of old pallets. There is another pile a short way off, and Callum points to it.

"What's that for?" he asks. Steven looks at it dismissively.

"Oh, that," he says. "That stuff won't float."

"How do you know?" asks Vicky.

Steven opens his mouth to answer but then stops, looking confused. "Well, to be honest," he says, "I'm not sure. I just...seem to *know,* somehow!"

"Steven," says Callum, "didn't you... Weren't you... Weren't you away somewhere? With Things-of... With..." He stops. Steven steps over to him.

"It's okay," he says. "I've got it too. You think something weird happened, but you can't say what, right?"

Callum nods, gratefully, and he notices Vicky and Craig are also nodding.

"It's been like this since they pulled you off the Mountain," Steven continues. "Everyone's got this weird, happy look about them, and they're all talking about Mountain spirits and things, but I... Well, *we* all think that something else was going on, but we can't say what!"

Craig pipes up. "It was something pretty scary, I think. I seem to remember wanting it to stop. But, well, everything seems fine now, so, you know... Probably nothing to worry about!"

And everything *does* seem fine. Better than fine, in fact. There are smiles on the faces of everyone in Skerrils, it's a gorgeous day, birds are singing, it's the holidays, and the whole day stretches out ahead of them. Callum gives a wee shudder, then grins.

"Right," he says, "let's build this boat!" But through his cheerfulness he cannot shake the feeling that, all the happiness and merriment aside, something indescribably precious and amazing has been lost.

Two hours later, with the boat half finished and looking unusually good, Callum excuses himself and heads home. He's very tired, still not recovered from his ordeal, and he needs a lie-down. On his way, he's both pleased and confused to see dozens of people out and about, heading to the beach, walking off up to the hill path, making the most of the day. There's a buzz about the wee town that Callum can't remember ever sensing before, as if Skerrils has somehow *woken up*.

It's nice, walking through the streets and seeing them busy, greeting lots of happy folk and agreeing that it is indeed a lovely day. Nice, but exhausting, and Callum is quite relieved to finally get home. He's straight up to his room and crashed out on the bed before Mum and Dad can even ask him how his morning's been.

Return

Later, much later, after a long and dreamless sleep, Callum is shoogled awake by his dad.

"We didn't want to wake you, son," he says, "but I thought you'd like to know—Papa got back this afternoon!"

Callum leaps out of bed with a shout of glee and thunders down the stairs and out the door, energy levels back to full tilt. The streets are still full of people, every spot of grass, from front gardens to roadside verges, play host to merry wee groups having picnics, playing cards, laughing and just generally getting together, and Callum has to offer breathless greetings to all of them as he runs round to Papa's cottage.

He's about to step in when the door opens and two elderly gentlemen come out, chuckling and slapping each other on the back. Callum has to step out their way to avoid being knocked over.

"Och, Gordon," says one, "you're a tonic, so you are!"

Papa appears at the door behind them, looking frail but happy. "Callum!" he says, delighted. "Gordon, Connor, you know my grandson, don't you?"

The two old men turn to Callum with warm smiles of recognition, but Callum can't quite place them. They do look familiar, but he's not sure why.

"Of course, of course," says the one called Gordon, "the hero of the hour! Nice to see you up and about, young Maxwell!"

It's only now that Callum realises it's Mr. MacQuarrie, all but unrecognisable without his customary scowl. Callum still can't place the other man, a dapper wee chap in a blazer, shirt and slacks, carrying a smart carved walking stick.

"Callum, of course," says the wee man in a funny, high-pitched voice. "You don't know all the good you've done, son," he says. "You've helped three stubborn old fools finally remember who they are!"

And that's when Callum realises this clean-shaven, well-turned-out little chap was, until three days ago, the fur-clad, cave-dwelling legend who pulled him out of the sea. He is too taken aback to speak, and Connor McKnight—*the Trog*—turns to Papa and says, "All that time, wasted. I should feel terrible about it, but, well, somehow I canny be sad on a day like this!"

Mr. MacQuarrie agrees, and with a final, cheerful cheerio to Papa and promises of more meetings to come, they head off down the road together, leaving Callum gawping after them.

Papa looks at him and chuckles. "Come in, Callum," he says. "I am feeling better, but I could do with a seat!"

And in minutes, they are in their old places, slurping tea and blethering away happily, Papa sooking contentedly on his pipe—"Against doctors' orders," he says with a mischievous smile.

Eventually, of course, the talk turns to the bizarre events of the summer so far, and Callum is quick to ask Papa what he makes of it all.

"Everyone's going on about the Mountain," he says, "but I don't even know how important that was! I mean, I can't actually remember even *seeing* the Mountain spirit, whatever it is! But I am sure I saw something, or someone... Things... Things-of... Well, amazing things! But if I try and think of them, to remember what they were like, it's like walking into a brick wall! Something's missing, Papa. Maybe the Mountain stayed where it should be, but something's gone, I *know* it has!"

Papa nods, thoughtfully. "Well, now Callum," he says, "have you had time to wonder whether or not you're better off without it, whatever it was?"

Callum looks at him blankly. "What do you mean?"

"Well, look at me, laddie. There's me had the first conversation with my two oldest friends in about seventy years! All this time, living in the same wee place, and we were kept from one another by *something*. Now, I do have the same feeling as you, Callum. I've come back to an emptier house, somehow. But the town...well, the town seems fuller and happier than I've ever seen it!"

Callum looks out the window at the sunny day outside, thinking of the merriment and energy that now seems to fill the town.

"Yes, but... Well, I'm glad everyone's so happy...but what about *us*?"

There is a moment of quiet, broken only by the ticking clock, as both Papa and Callum are lost in thoughts and vague, confusing memories. It is the old man who breaks the silence.

"I think, Callum, that we had a glimpse of something that was maybe *too much* for one or two people to handle. It seems to me there is a bigger, wider magic afoot, and *everyone* is touched by it. And listen, laddie—that is a wonderful thing.

"So, whatever private wonders we may have enjoyed before, well, perhaps it isn't too much for us to sacrifice them so that everyone can have a taste of *something*! Perhaps we can be grateful, you and I, for the things that we *have*, and not be too worried about the things we may have lost!"

Callum knows, as Callum often knows, that Papa is wise, and that Papa is right. He smiles.

"Okay!" he says.

And they laugh, and they chat, and they sup sweet tea as the golden day rolls on around them. Their talk is of hills and rivers and seas, of friends past and present, of birds and beasts and woods and streets, and it flows easily and perfectly between them like the scent of heather on a summer breeze.

But watching from the corner, listening, unnoticed and invisible,
     is a quick
       green
         figure,
           wrapped in a cloud
             of melancholy mischief.

the end

Glossary

Scottish people are fond of listing the many great and wonderful gifts they have given the world, and it is, indeed, an impressive list. Sadly, there's little hope of your average chap coming up with the next penicillin, or telephone, or blood-transfusion device, or cloned sheep. We can try, but it'll be a bit of a stretch.

Happily, there is a rather splendid secret treasure that we all still hold to ourselves and which it's always good to share with the wider world, in the shape of our living, musical and amusing *language*. Scots is a fond sister of English, and like English, it has dialects and variations up and down the country. Callum, like me and everyone I grew up with, hears Scots not as a broad, Robert Burns style discipline, but as a bit of occasional spice to the English he speaks, a bit of extra colour and texture if you like.

Below is a list of words from the story which might not be familiar to readers outside Scotland. There are enormous, groaning dictionaries filled with every Scots word ever uttered between the thirteenth century and now, but the short list below includes a few favourites. The only condition I used for including a word in the story (or, should I say, for not removing a word when one happened to pop out) was that it should be a word that I honestly use, or hear other people using, and not just something dug from the depths of these dictionaries.

Some of their meanings are obvious, as they are close cousins of their English counterparts—just as we are, as a people. Others tell of more far-flung friendships, with roots in Scandinavia, or Ireland, or languages so old that no-one even knows what they were anymore. I hope you enjoy looking through them, and I hope a couple might sneak their way into your everyday speech. A language that only exists on paper is no more use than an animal that only exists in a cage. Use these, enjoy them, and pass them on.

I should also confess that here and there, when the mood was upon me, I just made up a word. You should definitely try that too.

bahoukie – bum

birse – temper

blattering – pounding, usually talking about rain

bleezin – blazing. Also 'drunk', but not in a wholesome book like this.

blethering – gossiping, chatting

boaking – vomiting

bogging – disgusting

bowksome – disgusting again

bumbaiselt – bamboozled

byke – nest, usually a wasp's

clamjamfry – commotion, only moreso

clarty – dirty

contermaciousness – obstinacy, stubbornness

cowp – tip over

dinnae – don't

doitit – befuddled

dreich – dull and miserable, usually weather but sometimes a person

drookit – soaking

dumfounert – dumbfounded

dunted – hit

dwam – daydream, trance

eejit – idiot

fasherie – annoyance, irritation

feart – afraid

fleggit – also afraid

foosty – rotten

ghillie – gamekeeper

gie's peace – give us peace

glaikit – dopey

glaur – mud

glumphiness – grumpiness

gonny – going to

guddling – a method of catching trout with your bare hands

haar – a sea fog

heelster-gowdie – head-over-heels

hirple – limp

jandie – germ

keeking – peeking. It's better with a 'k', isn't it?

mislushious – malevolent

muckle – big

nyaffs – brats. Usually wee.

oxters – armpits

peching – panting

peely-wally – pale, pathetic

pliskie – mischievous

puddock – frog or toad

puggle – exhaust, tire-out

reeshling – rustling

rone pipes – drainpipes

scooshed – sprayed

scraichy – scratchy

shoogle – shake

selkies – seal spirits. Sometimes spelt 'silkies'.

skite – zoom

sleekit – ingratiating, sneaky

smeddum – character, or atmosphere

snell – chill, biting

sooks – sucks

spyugs – sparrows

stoory – dusty

stottering – staggering

swedges – big hearty chunks

tapselteerie – topsy-turvy

tattie-bogle – scarecrow

thrawn – perverse

tummeling – tumbling

uggsome – ugly

unchancy – unnerving, unsettling

whammlin – exactly as it sounds

wheesht – quiet, often used in the phrase '*Haud yer wheesht!*' which means 'shut-up'.

whin – gorse

yett – gate

Acknowledgements

Thanks to Karen Campbell for her encouragement and help as a mentor through the Wigtown Book Festival; to Floris Books for including Callum in the Kelpies shortlist, a much-needed confidence-booster; to Paul Magrs, Joan Lennon and the crew of the QQ Moniack Mhor; to Debbie McGowan, firstly for liking the book and secondly for dedicating her time and energy to editing it into a serviceable shape; and to Shell, long-suffering, firefighting, motivating superwoman.

Callum's Papa is, in a way, an amalgam of both my grandpas, Jock McClure and Dwight Bolinger, neither of whom could be in any way summed up in a wee book like this, and both of whom I remember with a heart full of gratitude and love.

About the Author

Alan McClure is a writer and musician based in Galloway, south-west Scotland. His creative output is eclectic and prolific, encompassing oral storytelling, poetry, songs, novels, short stories and audio sketches. He is a founding member of Lost Wasp Records, singer and chief songwriter with Alan & the Big Hand, occasional member of The Wee Folk Storytellers and a solo performer of growing repute. He is also a primary school teacher, a job which provides constant inspiration and ample opportunity for explaining and discovering through stories and songs.

By the Author

Medica Britanimalicum (Blurb, 2011)

Ross Bay and Other Poems (Blurb, 2011)

The Choices of Molly Fortune (Amazon, 2014)

Alternative Endings and Other Poems (Amazon 2014)

Other examples of Alan's music and writing can be found at www.alanmcclure.co.uk

Beaten Track Publishing

For more titles from Beaten Track Publishing,
please visit our website:

https://www.beatentrackpublishing.com

Thanks for reading!